Emily Har[illegible] UK – althoug[illegible] would prefer to live in the French Alps ... or Canada ... or anywhere that has several months of snow. Emily loves snow almost as much as she loves Christmas. Having worked in the City (London) for several years, Emily returned to her home town of Hastings where she spends her days writing ... and wondering if it will ever snow. You can contact her via her website, Facebook or Instagram.

There is also a Facebook group where fans can chat with Emily about her books, her writing day and life in general. Details can be found on Emily's website.

Author contacts:
www.emilyharvale.com
www.twitter.com/emilyharvale
www.facebook.com/emilyharvalewriter
www.instagram.com/emilyharvale

***

Scan the code above to see all Emily's books on Amazon

Also by this author

The Golf Widows' Club
Sailing Solo
Carole Singer's Christmas
Christmas Wishes
A Slippery Slope
The Perfect Christmas Plan
Be Mine
It Takes Two
Bells and Bows on Mistletoe Row

Lizzie Marshall series:
Highland Fling – book 1
Lizzie Marshall's Wedding – book 2

Goldebury Bay series:
Ninety Days of Summer – book 1
Ninety Steps to Summerhill – book 2
Ninety Days to Christmas – book 3

Hideaway Down series:
A Christmas Hideaway – book 1
Catch A Falling Star – book 2
Walking on Sunshine – book 3
Dancing in the Rain – book 4

Hall's Cross series
Deck the Halls – book 1
The Starlight Ball – book 2

Michaelmas Bay series
Christmas Secrets in Snowflake Cove – book 1
Blame it on the Moonlight – book 2

Lily Pond Lane series
The Cottage on Lily Pond Lane – four-part serial
Part One – New beginnings
Part Two – Summer secrets

Part Three – Autumn leaves
Part Four – Trick or treat
Christmas on Lily Pond Lane
Return to Lily Pond Lane
A Wedding on Lily Pond Lane
Secret Wishes and Summer Kisses on Lily Pond Lane

Wyntersleap series
Christmas at Wynter House – Book 1
New Beginnings at Wynter House – Book 2
A Wedding at Wynter House – Book 3
Love is in the Air – spin off

Merriment Bay series
Coming Home to Merriment Bay – Book 1
(four-part serial)
Part One – A Reunion
Part Two – Sparks Fly
Part Three – Christmas
Part Four – Starry Skies
Chasing Moonbeams in Merriment Bay – Book 2
Wedding Bells in Merriment Bay – Book 3

Seahorse Harbour series
Summer at my Sister's – book 1
Christmas at Aunt Elsie's – book 2
Just for Christmas – book 3
Tasty Treats at Seahorse Bites Café – book 4
Dreams and Schemes at The Seahorse Inn – book 5
Weddings and Reunions in Seahorse Harbour – book 6

Clementine Cove series
Christmas at Clementine Cove – book 1
Broken Hearts and Fresh Starts at Cove Café – book 2
Friendships Blossom in Clementine Cove – book 3

Norman Landing series
Saving Christmas – book 1
A not so secret Winter Wedding – book 2

ISBN 978-1-909917-77-4

Published by Crescent Gate Publishing

Print edition published worldwide 2023
E-edition published worldwide 2023

Cover design by JR and Emily Harvale

Emily Harvale

A not so secret Winter Wedding

CRESCENT GATE PUBLISHING

Acknowledgements

My grateful thanks go to the following:

Christina Harkness for her patience and care in editing this book.
My webmaster, David Cleworth who does so much more than website stuff.
My cover design team, JR.
Luke Brabants. Luke is a talented artist and can be found at: www.lukebrabants.com
My wonderful friends for their friendship and love. You know I love you all.
All the fabulous members of my Readers' Club. You help and support me in so many ways and I am truly grateful for your ongoing friendship. I wouldn't be where I am today without you.
My Twitter and Facebook friends, and fans of my Facebook author page. It's great to chat with you. You help to keep me (relatively) sane!

To view a map of Norman Landing visit

the maps page on my website

www.emilyharvale.com

To Jasmine and Ruby,
for being such sweethearts.

One

'I shouldn't have told you that!'

The wide-eyed look of horror on my new friend, Tori's face quickly turns to regret. She knocks back her fourth glass of bubbly and stares at me as if she's waiting for me to speak.

What can I say?

The secret she has just told me might very possibly change my life and there is no way I can ignore such news.

I'd hate to think my acting on it would upset her though. I only met her half an hour ago but I liked her the moment she introduced herself as Katie's best friend. I'd heard a lot about her from Katie. Not that I've known Katie long. About four weeks, that's all.

It's weird how some things happen, isn't it? As if they're meant to be. I wouldn't be here tonight if I hadn't met Katie.

And my brother, Aaron would still be miserable, if not for her.

Right now he and Katie are locked in one another's arms, staring into each other's eyes as if they are alone, and not surrounded by at least two hundred people in this fake but rather splendid, Winter Wonderland I helped to set up in Holy Trinity church hall.

This will sound ridiculous, I know, but either I've had too much to drink, or I've fallen into some sort of alternate reality where all my hopes and dreams finally start coming true. Everything is working out as I'd hoped. No, much better than I could have ever hoped, and that isn't usually how my life goes. Things rarely go to plan in my world. But they certainly are tonight. It's nothing short of a miracle.

Of course, it could all go to hell on the stroke of midnight. But it's Christmas Eve and Christmas is a time for miracles, isn't it?

Sorry. I'm babbling. I tend to do that when I'm nervous or excited. And right now, I'm a bit of both. I honestly can't believe how well things are going.

Let me bring you up to speed. I'm Meg Holt and I work for the local paper, *The Weekly Conqueror*, in the pretty seaside town of Norman Landing, which has been here since the time of William the Conqueror – the town, not the newspaper. Although who knows. Maybe the Saxons or the Normans had some sort of ancient version of a newspaper. History was never my strong point. I do know there's The Bayeux Tapestry. That tells the story of the Norman invasion and, like a newspaper, it's a type of report of the events of the time, only with scenes stitched in wool thread on linen cloth panels rather than words printed on pages of paper or accessed digitally on a screen.

Anyway, as I mentioned, I'm in Holy Trinity's church hall, attending the Christmas Eve party that's the result of a campaign I've been involved with, called Saving Christmas. I'm not one for blowing my own trumpet but I have to admit the campaign was a roaring success and this evening has been brilliant in every way possible.

The campaign wasn't my idea but it has done wonders for my career. It's brought me in contact with people I could never have connected with in the normal way of things. Everyone and anyone wanted to be involved and the campaign took on a life of its own. I've had meetings with some of the most powerful and influential people in the county – and not just the county – the country. Councillors, Members of Parliament, celebrities, local and national media including radio and TV, not just print. It's been amazing. And all because of Katie … and a fire at Conqueror's Court Care Home.

The fire happened in mid-December and the damage was extensive, but fortunately, no one was seriously injured. That was partly thanks to my brother, Aaron. He's a firefighter and, as always, he and the rest of the crew from Norman Landing Fire & Rescue, saved the day. And most of the building. But due to serious, safety concerns none of it could be occupied after the fire.

That meant all the elderly residents, both of the care home and also the flats in one of the wings of the once stately home, had to move to other accommodation. One of those residents was the grandmother of my new friend, Katie. Katie's the sister of Emma, my brother's next-door neighbour, and Katie is the one who had the brilliant idea to save Christmas for all the OAPs.

With me so far?

You probably don't need to know all this, except for the fact that it helps to explain why I'm so happy right now.

When Katie decided she needed to 'save Christmas' for her nan – who is actually called Nan – short for Nancy – and all the other elderly residents, she mentioned it to me and my brother, and that's how the campaign got started. She told me what she wanted to do and, me being me, I offered to help. The minute my bosses, Mr and Mrs Trewberry, the owners of *The Weekly Conqueror* heard about it, they came on board, and the thing kind of sky-rocketed from there. As I said, everyone wanted to be involved. It's at times like these when you realise just how wonderful humans can be.

So here we all are, on Christmas Eve in Holy Trinity church hall which has been transformed into a Winter Wonderland, enjoying a slap-up meal, washed down with more booze than is probably good for any of us, and having the time of our lives. Myself included.

Although for a time today I thought things had gone pear-shaped for Aaron. He and Katie had been getting on like a house on fire. Excuse the pun. I couldn't have been happier. Katie had recently been dumped by her long-term boyfriend and had come back to Norman Landing to stay at her sister Emma's house while Emma is in New York, on business. Aaron fell for Katie the minute they met, which was obvious to everyone except to him ... and to Katie.

Okay, maybe not the minute they met, but soon after. They had a bit of a disagreement when they first met.

Even when he realised how he felt, Aaron wouldn't admit it. Or tell Katie. This is my brother we're talking about and he's as stubborn as a mule when he wants to be. But he's suffered a personal tragedy and it's taken him a heck of a long time to get over it.

To be honest, I'm not sure he'll ever be over it, exactly. Losing your fiancée in a fire is enough to traumatise anyone, but for a firefighter who was off duty and away from the town at the time, it's worse, believe me. The 'if only I'd been there' guilt kicked in immediately. And it kept on kicking. Year after year.

Katie was a ray of hope. The first woman in a long time to put that special sort of smile back on my brother's face – the one that shows you are falling in love. And then today, her ex showed up and bloody well proposed to her on the front lawn of Emma's house ... in the snow.

I mean, come on!

Who does that?

I saw it all because I was with Katie at the time. And Aaron saw it too because he drove up just as Katie's ex, Cal, held out a beautiful bouquet and then went down on one knee and proposed.

I was so stunned I couldn't speak at first. Neither, it seemed, could Katie.

Nan – Katie's gran – and Donald who is Nan's 'special' friend, hurried out of Emma's front door. Ember – my brother's West Highland Terrier who I was looking after that morning, barked and growled at Cal, while Aaron stood, statue-like and opened-mouthed, staring at the scene before him.

Cal broke the awkward silence. 'Katie? I said I love you. I adore you. I want to spend the rest of my life with you. Will you please say yes, you'll be my wife?'

And to my horror, not to mention, Aaron's, she bloody well did!

'Yes. I'll marry you. Yes. I'll be your wife,' she said. Although, rather strangely, she seemed to be looking at Aaron at the time, not Cal.

Everything went a little crazy after that. Cal jumped up, tossed the bouquet to one side as if it had served its purpose, pulled Katie into his arms and kissed her, but from where I stood, it didn't look like she kissed him back. I shouted something I'd rather not repeat, and Ember tried to bite Cal on the ankle. Not that Cal appeared to notice. I was tempted to let Ember have a go at him but I wasn't sure what Cal might do so I gave Ember's lead a little tug and he came and stood beside me, still growling at Cal. My brother turned and marched towards his own front door, without a word.

Then things turned even more bizarre.

Katie pushed Cal away and called out to Aaron, but he ignored her. She called to him again and Aaron quickened his pace. He was running by the time he reached his front door. He raced inside and slammed it shut behind him.

Nan and Donald went to Katie.

'Are you sure about this, Katie love?' Nan said.

'Does this call for a celebration?' Donald asked, looking slightly unsure.

'What's going on?' Cal demanded, glaring from Katie to Aaron's house and back again.

'Let's get you inside,' Nan said, leading a somewhat bemused-looking Katie towards Emma's.

'Are you completely mad?' I asked, having found my voice. 'This guy dumped you, remember? Now you're going to marry him? Seriously? I hope you realise you've just broken my brother's heart.'

I don't think Katie heard me. She didn't respond in any way. Nan turned her head, gave me a wan smile and whispered, 'She's in shock.'

'Aren't we all?' I replied, sarcastically.

Cal went to follow his new fiancée but Nan shook her head at him. 'Leave her be for now, please Callum.'

'But ... we're engaged! Aren't we?' Cal glanced towards me as no one else answered.

'Oh shut up,' I said. 'Everything was going so well until you turned up. Just go away.'

To my surprise, he retrieved the bouquet from the snow-covered lawn, glowered at me and Ember and stomped off down the drive.

I hurried to Aaron's and found him slumped in an armchair, cradling a bottle of beer, despite the fact that it was morning.

He wasn't the only one who turned to alcohol. Tori told me half an hour ago that Katie did the same. The only difference being, my brother took a few sips of his and tossed it aside; Katie slugged down an entire bottle of bubbly, got completely sozzled and fell asleep.

So that's why she was late arriving to this shindig. I had wondered if she'd gone off to find Cal instead of attending this event we'd worked so hard to make happen.

I wanted to murder Katie for hurting Aaron. He went back into his shell and wouldn't talk about it all day, not even to Mum who can usually get him to open up about most things. But one of the entertainments for this event tonight was an auction for a date with some of the firefighters, one of whom was Aaron and there was no way he would let his fellow firefighters down, or the community in general. Aaron's sense of duty is legendary.

Nevertheless, I thought that, despite the massive success of the Saving Christmas campaign, me and my family were going to have a pretty miserable Christmas, with Aaron in a downward spiral, having lost yet another girlfriend. Although not in such a dramatic way as he lost his fiancée.

But Katie saved the day. She turned up forty minutes ago, arm in arm with Tori, who helped Katie onto a table near the door just as the bidding for a date with Aaron was about to start. I think Tori made a loud wolf whistle, but it could've been someone else. All eyes turned to Katie who yelled at the top of her voice that she'd pay whatever it took to get the date with Aaron because she loved him!

You could've blown me down with a feather. I don't think I've ever seen my brother so bemused and yet so happy at the same time. My dad was the auctioneer and he immediately proclaimed Katie the winner, providing she matched the highest bid for a previous candidate.

I'll admit I shed a tear or two. It was *sooooo* romantic. Aaron still looked dumbfounded as if he couldn't believe this could be happening, but everyone clapped and cheered as Katie hurried to the little stage at the end of the church hall. Even then, when she stood in front of him, Aaron seemed to be in a trance. I didn't hear what they said to one another because the cheering was so loud. That increased in volume once he finally pulled Katie into his arms and kissed her.

I could've kissed her myself, but Aaron seemed intent on being the only one to do that, so instead, I raised a glass of bubbly to them both and beamed at Dad and then at Mum, who was also looking decidedly weepy.

I thought the night couldn't get any better. But I was wrong.

Now Tori has just told me a secret – a secret that could change my life. A secret she could lose her job over if anyone finds out she's let the cat out of the bag.

She looks at me askance and then leans in: 'It is meant to be a secret. It's a secret winter wedding. Bugger. Don't tell anyone I've told you, will you, Meg?'

She puts one finger to her lips and makes a sort of shushing sound but it comes out more like a shrill whistle and a few people standing nearby turn and look at us.

I smile and link arms with Tori, leading her away somewhere quieter so that I can get more info about this 'secret winter wedding'. After all, it's not every day that a story like this lands in my lap. A story that could change my life. A story every media outlet in the land would kill for. I can see the pound notes falling into my arms ... and the job offers. This story is my ticket to the big leagues and there is no way I can let it pass me by.

Two

Nothing screams 'low key, secret event' quite like a wedding in a castle, does it? Especially as, according to Tori, it's one of those Bavarian fairy tale type things with all the turrets. But she assures me no one knows about this wedding, other than the couple's family and closest friends, Tori's boss, and Tori, and everyone has been sworn to secrecy.

'Damn it,' she says, stopping to refill her glass from the half-full bottle she grabs from the recently vacated table we were passing. More than half of the guests here tonight are old age pensioners, many of whom are over eighty, but most of whom are now on the dance floor, while the younger guests, like me and Tori are chatting or scrolling on their phones. Some are taking photos – which is what I should be doing. *The Weekly Conqueror* is planning a four-page spread for a special New Year edition and I'm providing the photos. But at this moment in time, this secret wedding is more important and besides, I've already taken enough to fill more than fifty pages and the New Year special won't be anywhere near that. I'm pretty sure at least one of the photos featured will be of Katie and Aaron kissing. I took several shots of that. I might even print one out and frame it tonight when I get home, and give it to Aaron as an extra little Christmas gift.

'Never tell me a secret,' Tori continues, now refilling my glass to the brim. 'I'm not very good at keeping them. Katie can vouch for that.' She pulls a face and grimaces as she puts the empty bottle back from where it came. That'll be a nice surprise for the guests at this table when they return from the dance floor. 'And you work for the local paper, don't you?'

I nod, trying to hide my excitement. Right now I could give a bottle of champagne a run for its money. I'm fit to pop my cork.

'Uh-huh,' I mumble, biting my lip to stop a delighted squeal from escaping. I take a deep breath and aim for calm, collected, professional, but I'm not totally convinced and from the expression on Tori's face, neither is she.

'Whatever,' she adds. 'The worst that can happen is I'll get the sack. And the way I feel right now, that might not be such a bad thing.'

I'm glad of her nonchalance. She's already told me the bride and groom to be don't want any press or publicity at all.

'And the thing is, Tori, I love my job. I really do. But, well, it's not my *dream* job. Working on this campaign has opened my eyes and given me a taste of what's out there. What I've been missing. What I could achieve if I only had a chance.'

'I know the feeling,' she says, gulping her drink. 'I'm nothing more than a glorified secretary, despite being executive p.a. to my plonker of a boss for the last five and a half years and probably more capable of doing his job than he is.' She smiles. 'That might be a bit of an exaggeration. But I can definitely do better than I am. If only someone would give me a chance ... and, maybe, if I weren't quite so lazy.'

I smile at her honesty. I should be honest too.

'Could you really lose your job if someone found out you'd let the cat out of the bag? Only ... this could be the chance I've been longing for. I write an advice column for brides, called *Aisle, Altar, Hymn.* It's a bit tongue-in-cheek but let's be honest, all women think they can change their man in some way, even if it's a tiny thing like making him put the lid back on the toothpaste, or using a coaster before putting his mug on the coffee table. It gives sensible, serious and useful advice too though. Sometimes.' I quirk a smile. 'My main job is a photojournalist. I covered the fire at Conqueror's Court and worked on the Saving Christmas campaign.'

'Yes. Katie's told me so much about you, which is why I wanted to get to know you myself. I feel as if we're already friends. I like the sound of your advice column. I'll have to read it. But to answer your question, yeah, I could lose my job.'

I frown. 'I'll possibly get to assist in covering the investigation into the running of Conqueror's Court and who and where the real owners are, but as exciting as that may be, that type of investigative journalism doesn't appeal to me. I fell into the job at the local paper. What I really wanted to do was work for one of those glossy, bridal magazines, going on photoshoots to exotic places, taking pictures of wonderful wedding venues, exquisite bridal gowns, and paradise honeymoon destinations, but those gigs are hard to come by, especially without any relevant experience.'

'Same as my job. I wanted to be the one to discover the best bands and stars of the future but you don't get to do that unless you know what you're doing.'

'Yeah. And how are you supposed to do that without getting the experience? It's a catch-22 situation.'

'Or a chicken and egg kind of thing.' Tori's glass hovers on her lips as she meets my eyes. 'So ... are you saying that breaking the story about Lucinda and Cody's upcoming wedding might open doors for you?'

I nod. 'It might even get me a seat at the table as a staffer at one of the magazines, or at the very least, a foot in the door as a freelancer.'

Tori shrugs and empties the contents of her glass. 'Then I say go for it. Only don't mention me, if possible. You could say a source close to the couple spilt the beans, couldn't you?' She grins. 'My boss might get the blame instead of me. He's really close to Lucinda and they're good friends, despite her having signed with another record label a couple of years ago.'

'I remember her changing labels. It was big news at the time.'

In case you've been on the planet Mars and don't know who Lucinda is, let's just say she's more famous than Adele, Madonna and Kylie, all rolled into one. You must know at least one of those icons of pop. Lucinda hit it big at the tender age of sixteen and you could decorate a house with her awards and platinum-selling hits. Lucinda puts the Star in Mega Star and then some, and she's still only twenty-five. People have been known to actually faint at the mention of her name. Can you believe that? I read it in the papers so I know it must be true. Sadly, I've never met her or written anything about her. But this may be my chance. You can see why I'm so excited, can't you?

'Yeah,' says Tori. 'My boss wasn't happy at first, but you don't end a friendship with someone like Lucinda, unless you're crazy. He's the one who discovered her and helped her career take off. They even dated for a while. Oh God! That's another secret I've let slip.' She shrugs. 'Oh well. They've been friends for years, which is why he's got an invite to the wedding. And does it even occur to him to ask me if I'd like to go? Nope. Selfish git. But who has to arrange his flights, transfers and accommodation? Yep. Me. I'm his executive p.a. not his bloody travel agent.'

Tori knocks back her fifth or sixth glass of bubbly, taken from a tray as one of the waiters passed. I've lost count.

'When is it?' I ask, as that has just occurred to me.

'The wedding? New Year's Eve.'

'New Year's Eve? This New Year?'

Tori furrows her brows. 'Yeah. It's all a bit rushed. Don't ask me why. But I suppose they thought the secret might get out if they planned it too far ahead. And they were right.' She quirks her mouth into a grin.

'Blimey. That doesn't give me much time. But I can see the headline now,' I say, drawing two imaginary parallel lines with my fingers. 'Pop icon – no – goddess, Lucinda Revere and Olympic downhill skier, Cody Clayton tie the knot in a Winter Wonderland setting in a fairy-tale castle in the Austrian Alps.' I smile. 'Okay. That needs work. But you get the gist.'

'I think it sounds good. Except the castle's in Germany, not Austria and it's technically the Bavarian Alps, not the Austrian Alps.'

'Germany?'

I try not to look too surprised but that doesn't sound quite so romantic as Austria somehow. Has anyone famous ever got married in Germany? I'm sure they have. I simply can't think of anyone right now. It doesn't seem to bother Tori.

'You could just say Alps, because aren't they all part of the same stretch of mountains that run for miles and miles?'

'I believe so. I may be wrong but I think they encompass seven central European countries. I just can't recall which ones. Austria, definitely.'

'And Germany,' Tori adds. 'Oooh! And Switzerland. I read that book about Heidi and her grandfather when I was at school.'

'Didn't everyone?' I smile and I count on my fingers. 'Okay. Austria, Germany, Switzerland. Then there's Italy, France and … erm … I can't remember the rest.'

'Having fun?' I turn to see Aaron and Katie, beaming like Cheshire cats as they come to stand with us.

'What are you two whispering about?' Katie asks, momentarily averting her adoring gaze from my brother.

'We're counting Alps,' Tori says, reaching out and hugging Katie. 'I would ask what you two have been doing, but as you've been doing it in front of everyone, there's really no point.' She winks at Aaron and a hint of crimson appears on Katie's cheeks.

'Counting Alps?' Aaron's dark brows furrow. 'What? Like the mountains, you mean?'

'Duh. Y-es, brother dear. Only not the actual mountains. Just the countries they encompass. There're seven but we can only recall five at the moment.' I reel them off, touching the outstretched fingers of my left hand with the tip of my right forefinger as I go.

'Actually, there're eight,' Aaron says. 'In addition to the ones you've mentioned, there's Liechtenstein, Monaco and Slovenia.'

'Really? Hmmm.' Tori and I exchange glances. No one likes a smart-arse. Except I do love my brother and I think Tori likes him too.

'Why are you counting them anyway?' Katie queries. 'It's Christmas Eve. You two should be having fun.'

I can't argue with that, but I do want to hear more about this secret – or now, not so secret, winter wedding that's taking place in a real Winter Wonderland in the Bavarian Alps, not a staged one like the one we're all standing in right now.

And then I have to find a flight to Germany, somewhere to stay, a cover story to hide who I am and why I'm there, and a way to get into this wedding, not to mention persuade my bosses to give me a few extra days off. Oh, and write something to go with all the photos I've taken tonight for the special New Year edition of *The Weekly Conqueror*.

Bearing in mind it's Christmas Day tomorrow and the wedding is on New Year's Eve, that gives me just a matter of days.

How hard can all that be?

Three

When we were kids, Aaron – who is eight years older than me, and I would be up by 5 a.m. on Christmas Day and on our hands and knees beneath the Christmas tree, snuffling like truffle hunting pigs, searching for our presents. By the time Aaron hit his teens, he was far too cool for that, but as I was so much younger, I still woke him at 5 a.m. and, because Aaron is Aaron, he would humour me and at least come downstairs and sit on the sofa while I searched. Now we're in our thirties and living in homes of our own and I can't remember the last time I was up at 5 a.m. on Christmas Day. Today, I was up at 4 a.m. having gone to bed at 1 a.m. but instead of searching for presents I've been scanning the internet looking for flights to Munich, the closest airport to the wedding venue, and places to stay in a place called Garmisch-Partenkirchen, which is where the castle is.

And I thought Norman Landing was a weird name for a town! But hey. Who am I to judge?

I've discovered that Garmisch-Partenkirchen is a ski resort and market town in southern Germany, and although I'd never heard of it until Tori told me about it last night – and I had to ask her to repeat it three times and search for it on my phone before I believed her – it's pretty famous. At least within the winter sports fraternity. It's nicknamed GaPa which is, thankfully, much easier to pronounce. GaPa was formerly two towns that united in 1935, according to the internet, and Garmisch is deemed to be the more fashionable part. Partenkirchen has cobblestone streets and exudes a more traditional Bavarian ambience. The best of both worlds in one town, I suppose.

Apparently, it's a well-known destination for skiing, ice skating and hiking and it sits at the junction of two valleys, the Loisach and the Partnach in the Bavarian Alps, near the foot of the Zugspitze, which is Germany's highest mountain. I Googled the place and from the photos I've seen, I must admit it does look rather pretty. I'm not a massive fan of heights but if I have time, I think I might take either the cogwheel train or a cable car up the mountain. There are two of those, it says. The **Zugspitze** and the

Gletscherbahn cable cars. There're a couple of restaurants near the top, and on the 2,962 metres high summit there's a golden cross. It looks beautiful in the photos. More impressively, there are scenic views of Germany, obviously, but also of Austria, Italy and Switzerland and a mind-blowing four hundred other mountain peaks. That's some view. Assuming you go on a good weather day and not when there's a blizzard outside like there is here in Norman Landing today.

It's just getting light outside now at 7.25 a.m. but I can't see farther than a few feet and although I'm looking forward to Christmas dinner at Mum and Dad's, I'm definitely not looking forward to the five-minute trudge through blinding snow to get there.

I suppose I ought to go and have a shower. I promised Mum I'd be there by 9.00 to help with all the preparations. If you knew my mum you'd know that she likes to have everything perfect on Christmas Day. Nothing odd about that; most people want Christmas Day to be perfect. Although let's be honest, when is any day ever truly perfect? Anyway, Mum

is one of those organised people who prepares everything ahead of time, so she doesn't usually need any help from me, but today is going to be different. There's a small spanner in the works.

Instead of Christmas dinner being enjoyed by just Mum, Dad, Aaron and me, not forgetting Ember, of course, last night, after Aaron and Katie got together, Mum invited Katie to join us. And not just Katie but also Nan. And Nan's friend, Donald. Luckily, Donald has to go to his daughter's for the day; an arrangement that had been agreed long before the fire at Conqueror's Court it seems, although Donald didn't appear that keen last night.

'I wish I could join you,' he said, 'but Mary doesn't like plans being changed and she can be a bit moody if that happens, especially at the last minute.'

I was tempted to say, 'so what?' but I was glad in a way. One less person to fight for the last roast potato.

But it still means we've got two more mouths to feed, two more places to set, and, more worryingly, two more presents to find and wrap and place beneath the tree. Plus, now Mum has a prospective new daughter-in-law to impress. Yes, I know Katie and Aaron only got together last night but believe me, just like me searching the internet for flights this morning, Mum will be sitting in bed with the pot of tea Dad has brought her, searching the John Lewis website for a wedding outfit and new hat. Mum is a big John Lewis fan. A shopping spree for Mum is a day spent in their London store.

After showering and putting on a dress – at Mum's insistence. The dress that is, not the shower, I pull on my over-the-knee boots and hunt for my longest coat.

'Wear something nice tomorrow,' Mum said as she kissed me on the cheek last night before she and Dad left the church hall. 'A dress. Not trousers.'

'Why? Are we travelling back in time to 1910, or something?' I remarked.

Mum simply smiled and rolled her eyes.

Unlike Donald's daughter, who sounds a bit of a kill-joy, Mum wouldn't really mind if I didn't wear a dress, but I love her to bits so I'm happy to go along with her little foibles. I just don't want my legs to freeze.

My phone beeps and as I take it from my handbag I see it's a text from Aaron. I'm surprised he's managed to drag himself away from Katie. I know for a fact she spent the night with him and whilst I'm delighted for them both, I must admit to being just a teensy bit envious. Not of Katie spending the night having sex with my brother, obviously. That would be gross. Just of the sex part. I can't remember the last time I had sex. Or a relationship. Or even a conversation with a man I found attractive.

'Happy Christmas!' the text says. 'Want a lift to Mum and Dad's later?'

Before I have time to respond, another text beeps.

'This is the best Christmas Day, ever.'

'Why's that?' I text back, grinning to myself.

'Funny,' comes the reply.

'Leaving now 'cos Mum needs me, so thanks, but see you there.'

I finally find my long coat and shrug it on as my phone beeps again.

'Katie's gone home to get dressed, so I can take you if that helps. Have you looked outside?'

'Yes. And yes to the lift. If you can see to drive.'

'Be there in five.'

He's at my door in four and a half minutes, which is pretty good going in this weather. It would've taken me longer than that just to clear the windscreen. Not that I would be mad enough to drive in a blizzard like this. Aaron's not at all fazed by the weather. He drives a fire engine in these conditions.

'Merry Christmas!' I say as I jump into his car. 'Talk about global warming, it's more like global freezing. How is it even snowing? It's cold enough to freeze a penguin.'

'Merry Christmas,' Aaron replies and I stare at him for a second or two. 'What? Is there something on my face?' He stretches across to look at his reflection in the rear-view mirror.

'Yes. It's called a massive smile and I don't remember the last time you wore one. I can't tell you how happy I am for you, Aaron. This sounds corny but you already look years younger.'

He beams at me. 'Really? I thought I'd look like crap this morning. I didn't get much sleep last night.' He nudges my elbow and the smile grows even broader.

I return his smile. 'Your face will split in two if you keep smiling like that. But it's so good to see and long may it continue.' I twist slightly in my seat. 'I didn't get much sleep last night either. Sadly, not for the same reason. Tori told me a secret. Something she shouldn't have but it's so big, Aaron that it might change my life.'

I briefly fill him in as he drives to Mum and Dad's and when we pull up in their drive, he turns and smiles at me.

'How can you say you haven't heard of GaPa?'

My brows furrow instinctively. 'Erm ... because I haven't. Or hadn't until last night.'

He lets out a dramatic and over the top sigh. 'Your problem is, you don't listen to me, Meg.'

'That's not true. I do.'

He shakes his head. 'If you did, you'd remember that, not only have I been to GaPa, but I know someone who lives there. And not only lives there. Happens to have a chalet smack-bang in the heart of the place. A large chalet with paying guests.'

I can literally feel my mouth dropping open and my eyes bulging. He's kidding. He must be. Things like this only happen in films. It's far too much of a coincidence to be believable.

'You're joking, right? But it's not funny, Aaron. This is serious. I'm serious.'

He sighs again and shoves the car door open. 'You see. You don't listen.' He gets out and peers at me, still smiling. 'Are you coming in?'

I clamber out after him, slamming the passenger door behind me and slipping in the snow. He grabs my arm to hold me upright and despite the snowflakes landing on my face I look up at him.

'Are you serious?'

He nods and leads me inside.

'Completely. Merry Christmas, Mum and Dad!'

Aaron's greeting brings our parents dashing into the hall. Dad is delighted to see us as is evident from his smile and hugs. Mum, not so much, it seems from the lines on her face as her brows knit together.

'What are you doing here, Aaron? Where's Katie? Is everything all right? I'm not ready. You're early.'

'Calm down, Mum.' Aaron hands his coat to Dad and wraps an arm around Mum's shoulders. 'Katie is at Emma's getting dressed. Everything is fantastic. I'm not staying. I've just given Meg a lift because of the weather and then I'll go and pick up Katie and Nan. We'll be back here at 10.30 as planned.'

Mum's relief is palpable and she places a hand on her chest.

'Oh thank goodness for that. I'd hate Katie and Nan to see the mess this place is in.'

Aaron and I exchange glances and burst out laughing.

'You'd need x-ray vision to find a speck of dust, Mum,' I say. 'The place is spotless as always.'

Mum tuts. 'You haven't seen the kitchen. Oh. Merry Christmas.' She kisses us both on our cheeks and finally smiles. 'Your father says I'm getting myself worked up and there's no need, but I want Katie and Nan to see us all at our best. You look lovely in that dress by the way, darling.'

'Thanks. I'm sure the kitchen's fine but I'll be there in just a sec. I need to have a quick chat with Aaron first.'

'I'll make coffee and bring you some mince pies,' Dad says as he and Mum head back towards the kitchen and Aaron and I walk into the living room.

'I'm telling you now, Aaron, if you're pulling my leg I'm going to break one of yours. When did you go to GaPa and who do you know who lives there?'

He flops onto the large L-shaped, navy blue sofa and puts his feet up on the pouffe, having removed his boots in the hall. I perch on the edge beside him so that I can look him in the eye. He stretches his arms along the sofa back and lets out the breath he's just taken in.

'You know Hugh.'

'The Hugh you work with? Yes of course.'

'And his wife, Greta?' he queries.

'Greta? Yes. The gorgeous blonde with the big boobs. She's Finnish.'

'She's German. Some journalist you are.'

'No she's not. We spent at least an hour talking about Finland at their barbecue last summer.'

Aaron laughs. 'That's true. You did. And she didn't know why, but she was far too polite to ask.'

'Oh come on. Are you honestly telling me Greta's German?'

He nods. 'Don't you remember how she and Hugh met? Me and some of the guys went to the Oktoberfest in Munich fifteen years ago. Greta was there with her friends and Hugh spilt beer all over her when he turned round and bumped into her. It was love at first sight and we didn't see either of them until the rest of us were leaving for the airport to come home. They were married six months later and guess where the ceremony was.'

'Munich?'

'Guess again.'

I sigh. 'GaPa.' I shake my head in disbelief. 'Seriously? But she lives here with

Hugh. So are you saying it's her parents who live in GaPa?'

'Her entire family. Parents, sister, brother, grandparents, cousins. The lot.'

'And they own a chalet? A chalet that I could, maybe, stay in?'

I'm getting excited. This is all clearly meant to be. I'm going to go to GaPa, get the inside scoop on the wedding of the year, and step into my dream job early in the New Year. I can hardly believe this is happening.

Aaron shrugs. 'I don't see why not. But it'll be expensive at this time of year. And they may be full. Shall I give Hugh a call and see what he can do?'

'Duh! Y-es, please! Why aren't you dialling the number right now?'

Four

I'm not sure if I've ever really believed in Fate, or Destiny, or whatever you want to call it, but the way things are going, I'm turning into a true believer. Everything is slotting into place like the cogs on a bicycle. Not that I've ridden a bike since I was a teenager. Do they still have cogs? I have no idea. The point is, it's all going so smoothly I'm convinced this is meant to be.

Even the one, small hiccup in my scheme turned out to be a bonus.

Aaron texted Hugh this morning and asked if he could spare a few minutes to talk – it is Christmas Day, after all, and people have other things to do than help facilitate my plans. I get that. Fortunately, Hugh said yes, and Aaron put the call on speaker. He explained to Hugh that I needed to spend a few days in GaPa in order to follow up on a potential story, but as this was supposed to be a secret wedding, Aaron didn't mention what the story was.

'And you wondered if Meg could stay at the chalet?' Hugh asked, catching on quickly. 'At any other time of year, I'd say that wouldn't be a problem, except it's ski season and the Christmas holidays. Not just that, the annual New Year's Ski Jump, which is part of the Four Hills Tournament takes place on January 1st at the Olympic Ski Jump in GaPa. On top of that, it's the venue for the men's slalom on January 4th in this heat of The Alpine Ski World Cup, so as you can imagine, GaPa is heaving with skiers, their teams, sports reporters and commentators, and thousands of fans. You'll be lucky to even find an empty cardboard box to sleep in at this time of year. But I'll see what I can do. I owe you, mate, so leave it with me.'

'So that's why they're getting married there,' I said, after Aaron hung up. 'I wondered why. Cody's a ski racer. They must be fitting in the wedding between events. That's not very romantic, but I can put a spin on it, I suppose.'

But when I did some research about Cody, the Four Hills Tournament, and The Alpine Ski World Cup, in between helping Mum prepare Christmas dinner, I discovered Cody was no longer competing in the World Championships this year after a nasty fall in his heat at the resort of Lake Louise in Canada in late November.

I also learnt that The World Cup starts in late October and there are several heats in various disciplines, like downhill, slalom, giant slalom and super G. Men and women compete separately and events are held in a number of different countries, right through until the presentation of the crystal globes at the season finale in mid-March.

I watched the video footage of Cody's fall on YouTube, several times. I'm not sure how the man is still walking, let alone getting married. He crashed at eighty kilometres an hour and resembled a ragdoll as he seemed to cartwheel head over heels – or skis – and slammed into the red safety netting, where his skis came off and he lay, twisted and half hanging in the netting. Miraculously, Cody only fractured his wrist. Within seconds of his fall, as people rushed to help, he managed to stand up.

Thankfully, it seems most ski racers walk away from such crashes, but there are a few who don't. Cody wasn't the only casualty of the day but every one of them walked away, much to my relief.

I honestly can't see the appeal of men and women speeding down mountains, and I wouldn't want to marry someone who did that. I'd be terrified for them every time they clipped on their skis.

But then again, my brother and other firefighters like him and Hugh go into burning buildings. You'd think that would terrify me and yet it doesn't. I suppose I've grown accustomed to it. Plus, I know he's good at his job. Perhaps, if you love a downhill ski racer, you become accustomed to that, too.

'Life is a lottery,' Aaron said as we were eating Christmas dinner and I was telling everyone about Cody and what I'd seen on YouTube. 'Accidents happen every day.'

A sombre expression fleetingly replaced the smile that had been on Aaron's face all morning, but as if she knew that he was probably thinking about what happened to his late fiancée, Katie lovingly squeezed his hand and moved a fraction closer, and Aaron's smile soon returned.

'This is hardly a pleasant topic of conversation for Christmas Day,' Mum said. 'Especially as we have guests.'

I had to admit, she was right, but I think Katie and Nan were enjoying themselves nonetheless.

Hugh phoned as we were all about to take an afternoon stroll to walk off the ginormous amount of food we'd eaten, and once again, Aaron placed the call on speaker.

'No room at the inn,' Hugh said, clearly amused by his comment, despite my disappointment. Well, it is Christmas Day so someone was bound to say it. 'But how do you feel about becoming a temporary seasonaire, Meg?'

'A what? That sounds like an infectious disease. But if it'll help me find a place to stay in GaPa, I'll do it. Only ... what's a seasonaire when it's at home?'

'It's what they call chalet staff these days. My parents-in-law don't really need additional staff but when I told them it was a favour for a mate, they said they could fit you in. They also said an extra pair of hands might prove useful, so I hope you don't mind a bit of cooking and cleaning. Probably more cleaning than anything because they have a chef. But you'll get bed and board in exchange. Oh, and a lift pass if you want one. They'll also throw in a few euros if you do help out.'

I looked at Aaron in disbelief as I checked what I'd heard. 'You're saying I'll get a place to sleep, free meals, a cover story, and I'll be paid! Miracles really do happen at Christmas.'

'And a ski lift pass,' Hugh added.

'That they can keep,' I said. 'I've been watching what can happen when you go down a mountain on skis.'

So now I'm back at home after a long but wonderful Christmas Day and I'm on the internet yet again, this time, booking flights to Munich departing on the 27th of December and returning on the 4th of January.

I've written the article for the New Year special edition of *The Weekly Conqueror* and sent it, and the photos, to my bosses, along with an email asking for time off and apologising for the short notice. I hadn't expected to hear back right away but I was thrilled to receive a quick response. Mrs Trewberry thanked me for the article and photos, told me they were fantastic as always, and said yes to the time off, adding that, after the exemplary work I had done for the Saving Christmas campaign, I had more than earnt it.

GaPa – here I come!

Five

"DELAYED"

The flashing sign sums up the story of my life so far so I'm not surprised to see my 8.50 a.m. flight to Munich is one of several flights delayed. There's still a lot of snow on the ground even though it hasn't snowed since Christmas Day but with the temperature hovering around freezing, ice is more of a problem now. Getting to Heathrow had been an adventure worthy of Scott of the Antarctic. But the smiling girl at the check-in desk assures me I'll be on my way as soon as they've de-iced the wings. That doesn't sound comforting but there's nothing I can do. I'm going nowhere fast. Yep. Definitely the story of my life.

I return her cheerful smile, albeit not so cheerfully, and stomp towards the nearest bar. At least I've checked in my suitcase which must be a promising sign but my carry-on is behaving like a wayward child ...

or a naughty puppy; the wheels keep catching making it difficult to pull along behind me. I stop and push it back and forth as if I'm vacuuming the floor and after a minute or two it seems fine.

Anxiety is setting in.

What am I doing?

Do I seriously believe I stand a chance of getting the scoop of the year?

Me? With my years of experience limited to reporting events in and around Norman Landing.

I must not talk myself out of this. Especially as all the stars seem to be aligned. Everything – apart from this delay, has worked out in my favour. Even the perfect cover story fell in my lap. And I'll be earning money. How cool is that?

But every minute I sit drinking coffee, is a minute that someone else might get to Lucinda and Cody's wedding venue before me and a scoop can only be won by one person. I want that person to be me, so time is of the essence. My flight should have landed in Munich at 11.50. It's a forty-minute trip from the airport to Munich's main station and from there it's a direct train to Garmisch-Partenkirchen station, taking an hour and twenty minutes, but the trains are hourly so if I miss one, that's another sixty minutes added to my journey. Even if things had gone smoothly, I wouldn't have arrived at Chalet Maria until around 4 p.m. at the earliest. Now I've got no idea when I'll arrive. I'd better call Maria and break the news.

I can't get that song from the film *The Sound of Music* out of my head. Mum and I watched it on Boxing Day and I've been singing it ever since. But as not only the chalet I'll be staying in, but also the owner of the chalet, are both called Maria, I suppose it's understandable. The fact that it's Germany, not Austria doesn't seem to register with my brain.

My carry-on is playing up again so I do the vacuuming routine once more. It worked last time and thankfully it does so now. I turn to continue on my way and some jerk smacks right into me.

'Owww!' I say, because it hurts. The guy is like a solid wall. Well ... a moving, solid wall. 'Look where you're going.'

'I'm so sorry,' the wall replies. 'Did I hurt you? I'm running late and I was scanning the departure board while talking on the phone. Not the best idea, I'll admit. I should've been looking where I was going.'

He reaches out his hand and briefly touches mine and as crazy as it sounds, a sizzle of electricity and heat runs right through me. I look into a pair of eyes as blue as a summer sky and a weather-tanned face so good-looking it takes my breath away. There's a slightly awkward, but at the same time utterly dazzling, smile on the generous and totally kissable mouth which opens slowly as our eyes lock, yet no words come forth. Love at first sight happens to people but I never thought it would happen to me, yet in that moment the cacophony of airport noise fades away to silence and the throngs of people disappear from view. If this were a film I swear there would be magic sparkles in the air between us, circling around us and pulling us together like our hearts were one and not two.

But that's just me being overly whimsical and stupidly romantic, having watched too many Christmas movies.

A lock of lustrous, deep brown hair flops across concern-furrowed dark straight brows giving this hot and uber-sexy man a momentary boy-like innocence. The firm jaw tenses and the spell is broken.

The buzz and shrill of the airport crowds in on us and the announcement blares from the tannoy.

'The delayed British Airways flight to Munich will now depart from gate–'

We interrupt the announcement in unison. 'That's my flight.'

He looks as surprised as I feel.

'Y-you're on the flight to Munich?' he asks, incredulity evident in his tone.

I nod as I struggle to find my voice. 'Uh-huh.'

Really? Is that all I can manage to say?

Now he looks uncomfortable and a little unsure of what to do or say. He glances towards the departure board and runs a hand through his hair.

'I ... need to grab a few things,' he says.

'Me too,' I lie.

The smile returns but it's not quite as dazzling this time.

'See you at the gate?'

I know what he really means is that he *won't* see me at the gate but I nod ... again.

'Uh-huh.'

What on earth is wrong with me? Can't I think of anything else to say?

'Have a good flight,' I add.

'You too,' he says, confirming the fact that a date at the departure gate is not happening, but managing to look disappointed enough to make me think he might be.

We stare at one another for a second or two more and then someone barges into him, spilling coffee over the back of his expensive looking jacket which has a logo on the front.

At least that wasn't me.

But when I see the owner of the coffee is a vivacious redhead with legs as long as a runway and her seemingly apologetic smile says, ‘Let me kiss it better’, I’m not quite as pleased. For some reason I recall how Hugh and Greta fell in love when he spilt his drink over her.

I turn and walk away. I can’t compete with that and the handsome man-wall appears to have already forgotten I was there.

Six

Greta's sister, Marielle is waiting for me on the concourse of Garmisch-Partenkirchen station which is just as well because my grasp of the German language is as good as my knowledge of Martian. Although luckily, everyone I've spoken to since landing at Munich airport seems to speak English, albeit by varying degrees, and the station isn't exactly huge, consisting of only five platforms.

Marielle's English is good, the sort of 'proper English' where she pronounces every word, but it makes her sound rather formal. Her quick hug takes me by surprise, as she greets me as if we're close friends, but it makes me feel as if we are. She's Greta's twin but they are not identical although you would instantly know they're related. She has the same ice white blonde hair, cupid's bow mouth, piercing blue eyes, and enviable figure that her heavy red coat can't hide.

'Your journey was good?' she asks, helping me with my troublesome luggage. It's not just my carry-on that's playing up now, my suitcase has joined in.

'Yes thanks,' I say, returning the genuinely warm and friendly smile but shivering as we step outside and the cold, early evening air hits me. It's colder than it was at home but the air feels different here. It's a dry, biting cold, not a damp and bitter cold that seeps into your bones like it does in England.

The delay only made my arrival here an hour late, and it's 5 p.m.

Except it's not, as the clock in the little tower on the station roof reminds me, Germany is an hour ahead which means it's 6 p.m. in GaPa.

I haven't eaten since breakfast. All I had at Heathrow was a coffee. Once I landed at Munich, I was so intent on getting here without a hitch that I completely forgot to eat, although I will confess I did also keep an eye out for the handsome man-wall. I hadn't seen him at the departure gate at Heathrow and there was no sign of him at Munich airport. I looked for him at the station, too, but I have no idea why. He had said he was going to Munich but not where he was going from there, if anywhere. Munich may have been his destination.

Maybe he and redhead were so wrapped up in one another, he missed the flight.

For some ridiculous reason, that thought bothers me far more than it should. I'll never see the man again, so why do I even care?

I see a Burger King restaurant forms part of the salmon-pink façade of the station and my stomach grumbles as I stare at it. I could kill for a burger and fries.

Marielle laughs. 'You are hungry?'

'Starving.' I laugh too.

'The chalet is minutes away. Mama has saved you some cake from the afternoon tea and dinner is at 7 p.m. for us, and 8 p.m. for guests. We eat a little earlier so we are not hungry during the evening when we are providing service, but you will not be working tonight. Mama says you will be tired.'

'Your mum is right,' I say, grateful that I can relax on my first night.

I get into Marielle's car and admire the view as we chat. I can't see that much because, of course, it's dark, but I can see we're surrounded by towering mountains and the place is absolutely magical.

The roads are surprisingly clear of snow and ice as are some of the pavements but all the buildings and homes are covered with a deep layer several centimetres thick.

Twinkling fairy lights are everywhere, as they are at home but everything here seems much cuter. I'd seen photos on the internet so I knew what to expect; the reality however is different and I gasp and gawp and point.

Many of the hotels, shops and other businesses have colourful façades beneath the gently sloping roofs and quite a lot have equally colourful wooden, window shutters. Most have window boxes, railings, or wooden balconies. I'd seen photos of the window boxes overflowing with geraniums and other flowers during the warmer months but even now they look lovely. Several of the wooden balconies are quite ornately carved.

Some of the buildings have beautifully painted frescoes depicting religious scenes or local life and I turn my head from side to side trying to see each one but there are far too many. I'll have to go for a walk around and take plenty of photos. Mum and Dad would love it here.

'This is your first time in Germany?' Marielle asks.

'It is. It's even more beautiful than I'd imagined.'

'It is a pity that there are so many clouds tonight and you cannot see the moon. That is a marvellous sight. I never tire of it. But the forecast for tomorrow is clear and seeing your first sunrise over the mountains will be a joy.'

'Sunrise? I assume that means we'll be getting up very early.'

'Not a morning person?'

'Not especially. But I can be.' I beam at her. 'I'm so grateful for this, Marielle. Your parents are very kind to take me in and give me this opportunity.'

'It is for a story? Papa says you are a journalist.'

'A photojournalist for my local paper, yes. But my dream is to work for a magazine and I'm hoping this story will ... help me achieve my goal.'

I don't want to give away too much. I know this is Greta's family and I have no doubt they're as lovely as Greta is, but I'm not sure who knows what about this secret winter wedding so for now I'll play my cards close to my chest.

'It is good to have a dream,' says Marielle, 'and I am pleased that we can help.'

Before I know it we appear to have left the town and are climbing upwards via a steep and winding road with trees either side, their branches heavy with snow. I turn slightly and see glimpses of the lights below between the trees but even though it's only minutes away, the GaPa now seems a long way down. The car windows are obviously closed, but I can hear the silence. That sounds crazy, I suppose, but it's true. The bustle of the town has gone and other than the noise of the engine, there's nothing. I press the button to open the window a fraction to check – but quickly close it.

'Blimey! It's cold out there.' I shiver for effect and smile at Marielle. 'Is it always this quiet here?'

Marielle smiles back. 'Yes. You will quickly grow accustomed to the quiet. But it will not last for long. We will soon be there and our guests can be very noisy.' She points ahead. 'There is Chalet Maria.'

I can see some lights flickering through the trees in the distance but not the chalet itself.

'How many guests do you have?'

'Twenty. The chalet is divided into two parts, although they are not equal in size. There are ten en-suite guest bedrooms, a dining room and a sitting room for them. Then there is the family section, with four en-suite bedrooms, a large kitchen, a dining room and a sitting room for us. Mama and Papa converted the chalet to keep the guests separate from the family. "Guests are wonderful," Mama says, "but family life is precious." There is a door between the two sections, of course.' She laughs. 'We could not cook meals in the kitchen and then have to carry them outside. On the ground floor, there is a ski room, a laundry room and a steam room and outside there is a hot tub. The chalet is a ski-in, ski-out property.'

I'm picturing the steam room and hot tub when her last sentence hits home.

'Ski-in, ski-out? Are you saying we can't drive to the front door? I don't ski, so I'll have to walk.'

Marielle snorts with laughter. 'You do not know much about winter sports. I am sorry. I should not laugh. Do not worry. It simply means that guests can ski the moment they step outside and do not need to walk to the lifts. They can also ski directly back to the chalet. For skiers and snowboarders, that is a bonus and it makes our chalet more desirable. We will drive to the front door.'

I let out a sigh and grin apologetically. 'Phew! That's a relief. Sorry. I've clearly got a lot to learn about winter sports.'

'If you like, I can give you a few skiing or snowboarding lessons. Or my brother Otto, perhaps. He is a ski and snowboard instructor.'

'Is he? Oh yes. I remember Greta telling us.' I also vaguely remember seeing a photo of Otto once and thinking he was good-looking. I'm not sure I particularly want to learn how to ski or snowboard but I wouldn't mind spending some one-on-one time with

Otto. 'Thank you. That would be lovely. As long as we can stay on the beginner's slopes. I've seen what can happen on the steeper ones.'

She grins. 'There is also cross-country skiing. The terrain tends to be flatter. Or snowshoeing. And there are other winter sports here, like winter hiking, ice skating or sledging. Or if you prefer something more tranquil there are horse-drawn carriage rides, hot air balloon flights or paragliding. We have several swimming complexes and wellness centres. Or to simply relax, there are spas.'

'I really like the sound of the spas,' I say, grinning back.

Marielle easily manoeuvres the car around the sharpest bend I've ever seen and then another and suddenly, not only can I see Chalet Maria straight ahead, I can also see another even larger chalet a short distance away, but more importantly, I can see a castle.

It's nestled amongst more trees and majestic mountains, but it sits tall and proud and magnificent, the turrets clearly visible, being lit up from below. I gasp as if all the breath has been sucked out of me ... because in a way, it has. I have never seen anything so breath-takingly beautiful in my life. And now

I understand completely why Lucinda and Cody want to hold their wedding here.

Who wouldn't?

Tori has already told me the castle is called Ritterherzburg which apparently translates to Knight's Heart Castle. Personally, I think it sounds more romantic in English but I don't tell Marielle that.

'It is one of the oldest castles in Germany,' Marielle says, 'and is still lived in by the Ritter family, the descendants of the knight who had it built. Much of it is private but some of the rooms can be visited by tourists, and weddings are performed in the chapel but they are expensive and so it is mainly for a select few.'

'Does it accommodate guests?'

She shakes her head. 'No. Unless they are friends of the family.'

Are Lucinda and Cody friends of the family? If not, it means they must be staying elsewhere. Unless the owners have made an exception. I can't imagine anybody saying no to Lucinda. But maybe if you own a castle you can say no to anyone.

'So ... if you want to have your wedding there, you have to stay somewhere else?'

'Yes. A few couples have stayed at Chalet Maria because we are so close but the rich and famous will stay at the chalet you can see amongst those trees. That's Schloss Schatten.'

'Schloss Schatten?' I laugh. The name appeals to my childish sense of humour.

'I know what you are thinking.' Marielle laughs too. 'But it translates to Castle Shadow. At sunrise it is in the shadow of the castle.' We pull up outside Chalet Maria and she turns and smiles at me. 'Welcome to our home.'

Seven

Chalet Maria is as beautiful as any of the buildings I have seen so far. It is four storeys high, three of which have ornately carved wooden balconies in front of large windows from which warm amber lights shine out, guarded by forest green shutters. The eaves below the snow-covered, gently sloping roof are adorned with twinkling white fairy lights, as are the balconies and the two pine trees either side of the massive wooden double doors of the entrance. The façade of the chalet is painted the palest lemon which perfectly complements the dark wood of the balconies and the forest green shutters.

Inside is equally beautiful and with its abundance of ornately carved wooden posts and beams it has a traditional 'olde worlde' Bavarian charm, yet at the same time it is stylish and modern.

Glad to be in the warm, I follow Marielle up a flight of wooden stairs, having taken a quick peek into the ski room, steam room and laundry area and made a mental note of which door leads outside to the hot tub.

The stairs open into a wide hallway which has a large door to the left and a matching door to the right. Bookshelves line the rest of the hallway at the end of which there is a huge picture window with the comfiest looking window seat I've ever seen. There's space for two or three people to sit on the deep padded cushions, or for one person to stretch out languorously and simply admire what I can see is a spectacular view, even though its dark outside.

Marielle opens the door to the right and I find myself in another hallway. This one is slightly smaller than the last but with more doors, and in place of the window seat at the end, there's a further flight of stairs.

'We will leave our coats and boots here,' she says, pointing to a cloakroom. 'Do you have slippers? Or any other shoes?'

'In my suitcase,' I say, taking off my coat and pulling off my boots. 'But I can walk around in my socks for now, if that's okay.'

'Of course. You are sleeping in Greta's old room which is next door to mine on the top floor but we will leave your luggage here and go and meet my family and get you something to eat and drink.'

I smile before taking a deep breath and following Marielle. I can't wait to meet her family but I'm also a little anxious. I hope they don't ask me too many questions about the story I'm here for, because I don't want to lie to them but I'm not sure if I can tell them the truth.

Marielle opens the first door in a row of three along the hallway and I find myself in a spacious but cosy sitting room. My feet sink into the soft rugs scattered on the wood floor and the heat from a super-sized wood burning stove in the centre of the front wall hits me. The wood panelled walls are adorned with both family and scenic photos, together with several still-life paintings and some of local vistas. There are two large French windows either side of the wood burner, leading out onto one of the wooden balconies I'd seen earlier. The wall opposite the door has more large windows and some armchairs and occasional chairs are dotted in front of those as if positioned to admire the views. In addition, there are two huge sofas, a sideboard, some shelves along another wall, and a variety of side tables and table lamps. There are open drapes at the windows, as if they are there purely for decorative purposes and not to shut out the night, or keep the heat in.

'Make yourself at home,' Marielle says. 'I will tell Mama and Papa you are here.'

Before she has a chance to move, I hear cheerful voices in the hall and a tall, elegant, smartly dressed woman with blonde hair in a plaited chignon and a warm smile on her face marches in. She's followed by a mountain of a man who vaguely resembles a bear, especially with his dark brown, spiky haircut. He's wearing brown trousers, a beige open-necked shirt, a brown cardigan, and a smile as warm as the woman's.

'Welcome, Meg. I am Maria, and this is my husband, Gunter.' She greets me with a hug just as Marielle had done.

'It's so good to meet you,' I say. 'Thank you for letting me stay here. I don't know anything about being a seasonaire, I'm afraid, but I'm a hard worker and a fast learner.'

'Marielle will show you all you need to know,' Maria says, still smiling as she waves a hand in the air as if brushing that problem aside. 'You must be tired and hungry. Dinner will be in forty minutes but we will bring you cake and hot chocolate. Our home is yours. You will tell us if there is anything you need?'

'Yes,' I nod. 'Thank you.'

Gunter hugs me then and I prepare for my breath to be crushed out of me but the man is as gentle as a lamb.

'Ah! Here is Otto.'

Maria turns to the door as a tall, handsome man with golden hair, the face of an angel, the body of a demi-god, a film star smile and a hint of devilment in his strikingly blue eyes, saunters in. He's wearing black jeans and a black polo neck sweater and he looks every inch the ski instructor ... or maybe a secret agent.

Sadly, he's the only one who doesn't hug me, instead he holds out his hand and shakes mine in a formal greeting.

'You are Meg?'

He sounds surprised but I don't see why he would be. Heat rushes to my cheeks as he scans me up and down.

Marielle says something to him in German and then apologises to me.

'I am sorry. We must speak only English. I was asking Otto why he is late.'

'Please don't apologise,' I say. 'I'm the one who should do that. Unfortunately, I don't speak one word of German though.'

'Marielle is correct,' Otto says, his voice almost as dreamy as the rest of him. 'We must speak English when we are with you. I am late because there was an accident on the slopes. No one is seriously injured but three people have been taken to hospital with broken bones. One of them is Konrad, my friend.'

He obviously added that last bit for me because as soon as he said the name, everyone else in the room gasped, so they all know Konrad. They quickly revert to their native tongue and it's a few seconds before Otto smiles at me.

'Once again we must apologise. Konrad is a close friend and everyone was asking how he is.'

'Please,' I say, raising my hands in the air. 'Don't apologise. But how is he?'

Otto's smile broadens and he bows his head to me in an oddly old-fashioned gesture.

'He is well, thank you, but his arm is broken. A skier who should have known better was on a black run with ability to only ski a blue – if that. Konrad saved him from ... hurtling – yes? That is correct? Or flying ... from the edge of a sheer drop. Not all the pistes have barriers but they are all clearly marked and there are many warning signs. The man lost control and did not know how to stop.' Otto shakes his head. 'It could have been far worse.'

'Blimey. Why didn't he just fall over? Not over the edge. I mean, why didn't he fall down to stop himself?'

'Fear,' Gunter says. 'It is sometimes difficult to fall if you are out of control and at speed. And people do not think when panic takes hold.'

'Papa is correct,' Otto says. 'Do you ski?'

'No. And the more I hear about it, the less keen I am to try.'

Eight

I showered and dressed by 6.30 a.m. in plenty of time to see the 8 a.m. sunrise, which is later than I expected. I've also eaten breakfast – and that was a surprise.

We ate in the family dining room – where we had dinner last night – and I couldn't believe my eyes.

'There is a German proverb,' Gunter said: 'Eat your breakfast like an emperor, lunch like a king and dine like a pauper.'

'Breakfast has always been one the most important meals,' added Maria.

Although we had definitely *not* dined like paupers last night, they weren't kidding about breakfast.

The dining table was brimming over with choice. There were pots of tea, coffee and hot chocolate, along with jugs of fruit juices. Several pretty plates held slices of fresh, crusty or toasted bread and bread rolls. Butter and margarine sat in separate dishes, and there were pots of marmalade, jams and chocolate and hazelnut spread together with locally sourced honey. Plates of cheese, hard and soft boiled eggs, finely sliced meats and wurst – which is sausage, added to the selection. There was also Muesli, fresh fruit and yogurt. But my favourite things were the plates of finely sliced stollen, and also the apple and cinnamon pancakes, made with fresh apples and served with a sweet cinnamon sauce on top.

I was slightly taken aback when Otto filled a bread roll with butter, a slice of Emmental cheese and a slather of honey and ate that odd combination at the same time as a hard-boiled egg. But Gunter did the same, except he had raspberry jam instead of honey, which to me seemed even more weird.

I'm not sure how I managed to stand up after the amount of delicious food I ate but I did. Not only that, I helped Marielle set the tables in the guest dining room, learnt how to make the cinnamon sauce for those scrumptious apple pancakes, and assisted Maria and Marielle with various kitchen chores.

Gunter and Otto chopped more wood for the stoves and carried out other tasks, like fixing a leaking tap, a squeaky door, and a wobbly chair.

The chalet was a hive of industry but it seemed to run like clockwork and by the time the sun was ready to rise, all the jobs were done and twenty guests drifted down to partake in their own breakfast feasts.

Having been told by Maria that I could take a coffee break, I wandered into the dining room and stood in front of the windows to see if Marielle is right about the sunrise being joyful.

Otto now comes and stands beside me, so close I can smell the shower gel he used this morning. Or maybe it's his aftershave. It has that sort of soapy fresh aroma and it conjures up an image of him naked save for a thick white towel wrapped around his hips, his golden hair dripping water down his bare torso...

I shake myself out of that daydream but I cast a surreptitious glance in his direction and gasp as our eyes meet. He was looking at me! As foolish as it sounds, I can't help wondering if he was having a similar daydream about me.

Huh! I should be so lucky.

I hastily turn my attention back to the sunrise and my thoughts about Otto quickly fade as varying hues of pink and red and gold flit across the sky behind the snow-covered mountains.

'It's stunningly beautiful,' I say.

'Yes,' he says, in that soft and dreamy voice of his. 'Very beautiful.'

I get the distinct feeling he's still looking at me but I daren't check, because if I do – and he is – I may well throw myself at him.

I concentrate on the sunrise and within a few seconds I'm completely mesmerised by its beauty. The sky is alight with colour and the tips of the mountains are now golden instead of white as the rays of the sun sweep over them. For a moment or two it seems as if the tops of the trees are on fire and as the sunbeams land on Ritterherzburg, it's like the castle has taken centre stage and is actually gleaming with pride in the spotlight.

As I watch, the castle's shadow forms a dark path on the snow and it creeps towards the forest of trees amongst which Schloss Schatten is nestled. From where I'm standing I can see the large sloping roof and the upper floors of the chalet and the place is definitely cast in the castle's shadow, so it's very aptly named.

Within a few minutes more, the sun clears the mountain peaks and spreads its glow over Chalet Maria and the rest of the mountains and the valleys below, including the town of GaPa. Only a small area of the town is visible from the dining room window but from the front of the chalet and the sitting room, most of it will be in view. Last night, from my bedroom window on the top floor, I saw all the lights of GaPa, shining like a magical fairy grotto; the area I can see now, is bathed in a golden hue.

There isn't a single cloud in the sky. It's going to be a beautiful, sunny day.

I take a deep breath as if I'm trying to breathe in the sunshine and it's only then that I remember Otto is beside me. I also remember my coffee is getting cold. I gulp down the warm contents of my mug and try to think of something to say.

I can see, over the rim of my mug, Otto is smiling at me.

What is he thinking?

A smile curves the corners of his mouth and lights up his blue eyes.

'Meg?' he says, as I hold my breath. 'Would you like me to give you a skiing lesson today?'

Nine

I wasn't particularly tempted by Otto's offer, especially when he told me I could join one of his 'scheduled' classes, but when he added that we could then have lunch together and afterwards he could give me some one-on-one tuition, I almost said yes.

I had to remind myself why I was here. It wasn't to learn to ski and it wasn't to spend time with a handsome ski instructor. I was here to get an inside scoop on the wedding of the year.

I now tell myself that once more, as I look at my reflection in the full-length mirror in the hall.

'I am here to get an inside scoop on the wedding of the year.'

Today is the 28th and Lucinda and Cody's wedding is only a few days away. I have to find out where they are staying, find a way to get into the wedding and find a way to take lots of photos of the happy couple, all without them knowing. If they discover what I'm doing, I might be escorted to the airport by Lucinda's security team. I've seen a couple of videos on YouTube of her team of hunky security men 'persuading' paparazzi to move on. I rather like my bones as they are, so I need to be careful, canny, and quick.

I am also pretending to be a seasonaire, so I ought to do some more work. The guest rooms won't clean themselves and, although both Maria and Marielle have told me they can manage if I want to have a wander around GaPa and get my bearings, it doesn't feel right to skive off. Particularly as I've already eaten my own body weight in food and I'm staying here for free.

My brown hair is coming loose from the ponytail I tied it into this morning so I wrap the scrunchie a little tighter, take a deep breath and head off to clean my first loo.

I'm not a big fan of housework at the best of times so I didn't think I'd enjoy cleaning other people's rooms but once I get to grips with the routine Marielle has shown me, it's not as bad as I'd thought.

I'm now finishing off my fourth room and it's the messiest bathroom yet. There're more beauty products in this en-suite than I've seen on many a cosmetics counter. Every flat surface is piled high with cleansers, moisturisers, serums, foundations, eye shadows and more. I accept, as the room is being shared by two young women, there will be at least two of everything, but who on earth needs six different serums? I don't even have one. But then again I've never really bothered with expensive beauty products. My mum is in her sixties yet she has the complexion of a forty-year-old, and she only uses Astral cream and always has. If it's good enough for my mum – and for Joanna Lumley, it's good enough for me.

These two women could buy their own ski chalet with the amount they must've spent on all this stuff.

I try to clean around it all as best I can but I accidently knock one tub of eye-wateringly expensive-looking serum into the loo. I quickly fish it out, wipe it dry and put it back. Thank heavens the lid was on tight; I'll have to hope the label doesn't peel off. I'm more careful as I clean around the rest, so this room takes me twice as long to finish as it should and when Marielle comes to check if I'm okay, I tell her what I've done.

She snorts with laughter and shakes her head. 'I did the same yesterday to that one.' She points to another tub of cream. 'The label states it contains gold leaf. The lid was not on tight so it now also contains toilet water. Clean, toilet water, I am thankful to say.'

I can't help but laugh even though I don't suppose the guest would find it funny.

It's almost lunchtime now and I'm astonished my tummy is rumbling. How can I be feeling peckish? People say, "the more you eat, the more you want", and I suppose it must be true. But I have worked off several hundred calories this morning, so I'm not too worried.

Lunch consists of more freshly baked bread, a potato salad containing sausage, and soup ... also containing sausage. Sausage seems to be a firm favourite with this family. Otto doesn't join us, so it's only Marielle, Maria, Gunter and me.

'Can anyone walk in the nearby forest, or is it owned by Schloss Schatten?' I giggle as I say the name; I just can't help it.

'It is public land,' Gunter says. 'Only the garden of the chalet and the swimming pool are private but the boundaries are clearly marked.'

'I'd like to take some photos,' I say. 'And what about the castle? I know you told me, Marielle, that some of the rooms can be visited by tourists, and weddings are performed in the chapel. Is that open to the public at this time of year?'

'Yes,' Marielle says. 'On certain days. Of which today is one, I am sure. Yes, Mama?' Maria nods in confirmation but continues eating her soup as Marielle continues. 'You can take the road, or there is a path through the forest. Tickets can be purchased at the castle gate. Would you like me to go with you?'

'That's very kind. But I'm happy to go on my own. I'm sure you've been there loads of times. Besides, I tend to get a bit carried away when I'm taking photos and I'd hate for you to be bored. What time should I be back to help with afternoon tea?'

Marielle smiles but it's Maria who replies.

'That is at 4 p.m. but there is no need for you to help today. It is only bread and jams and cakes, and Marielle and I can manage easily. We will save you some cake.' She winks at me.

'Are you sure? If so, I'll be back in plenty of time to help with dinner, both for us and the guests.'

They have a chef who cooks dinner; I met him last night. His name is Bruno and he has a mop of wild, black hair, a ready smile and a voice that booms out commands. He dashes around the kitchen as if he's on roller skates, weaving in and out of anyone in his way. But there's still plenty of jobs to be done to prepare the meals for the family – and me, and the three-course meal for the guests.

And then there's service, plus the clearing up that needs to be done after that.

Marielle nods once. 'We will begin around 6 p.m., eat at 7 p.m. as we did last night, and then serve the guests an hour later.'

'I'll be home by 5 p.m. at the latest,' I say. 'Thank you for this delicious lunch. I'll stay and help wash up and then I'll get changed and go to the castle.'

'It is a pleasure,' says Maria. 'But we will clear the plates. Enjoy your afternoon.'

I don't need to be told twice.

Ten

The only sounds I hear, as I walk in the dappled sunshine through the forest, are the crunch my boots make with each step I take and the occasional 'plop-thrump' as a clump of melting snow falls from the branches of the pine trees and thuds into the otherwise pristine blanket of white, either side of me.

I'm taking the footpath to the castle, which seems to be quite well-trodden as the snow beneath my feet is more compacted. The path passes near Schloss Schatten so I suppose people come and go this way.

Nevertheless, it's hard to believe I'm anywhere near a famous winter sports resort, let alone one of the venues for two big events in the winter sports calendar.

Not that I knew a thing about any of this until a few days ago, but thousands of people did, and a large number of them are in GaPa and the surrounding areas right now.

Not forgetting, it's also Christmas week and hundreds are here for their Christmas and New Year holidays.

From time to time I do hear a sort of background thrum and I've heard a chorus of muffled cheers a couple of times, but other than that I'm surrounded by silence.

That is until two large, barking beasts come charging towards me out of nowhere.

I stop in my tracks and stare ahead, uncertain of what I should do. I'm not sure if they are dogs – or wolves ... but wolves howl, don't they? Their thick dark grey and white fur gives no clues. Do I run? Or do I stand my ground? They're heading in my direction and they're moving fairly fast.

And yet there's something about them that makes me think they don't mean me any harm. I still have doubts, until I hear a deep voice in the distance and both beasts stop and briefly look back. Then they observe me with piercing blue eyes and I realise they might be Huskies.

A man is now running towards them and he calls out, 'Ares! Beau! Wait.' He's still a fair distance away but is closing fast. 'I'm so sorry,' he shouts. 'They won't hurt you. Don't be frightened.'

As if to prove his point, one of them leaps up and down on the bank of snow at the side of the footpath. The other dives headlong into a deep pile and then rolls over on his back and wiggles his body to and fro as if he's attempting to make the doggie equivalent of some sort of snow angel.

'I'm not,' I shout back, laughing at their antics. 'At least, now I know they're not wolves.'

The man covers the ground between us and there's something about him that rings a bell in my memory. I'm sure I've seen him before, but it's only when he's a few feet from me that I recognise who he is. It seems he recognises me too.

'It's you!' he says, coming to a quick stop less than three feet away.

'It's me?' I try to play it cool by sounding casual yet confused.

'Heathrow airport.'

'Erm, no. My name is Meg, not Heathrow airport.' It sounded funnier in my head, but I'm pleased to see his lips quirk into a grin.

It fades as fast. 'You don't remember. Why would you?' He looks over his shoulder at the dogs who are now play fighting one another. 'I hope they didn't scare you. I should've kept them on their leads but I didn't think many people used this footpath.'

'It seems well-trodden to me,' I say. That sounds rude so I add, 'But I didn't expect to see anyone either.' And now I'm feeling guilty. 'I do remember seeing you at Heathrow airport. I'm surprised you remember me. Especially after having coffee spilt on you by that stunning redhead.'

I should've stopped at 'airport'. I hadn't meant to say the rest.

His brows furrow momentarily as our eyes lock, and it's as if there's something in the air between us. A frisson of electricity. I recall the thrill of something similar when he touched my hand at the airport. He's looking at me as if he wants to ask a million questions but he starts with one.

'Is that why you walked away? When I looked back, you were gone.'

'I ... had a flight to catch.'

'I only just made it. I was going to look for you on the plane...' His voice trails off and he seems embarrassed as my own heart skips a beat. He coughs. 'Are you staying in GaPa?'

'Erm ... Yes. At Chalet Maria.'

I turn and point through the trees towards the chalet and try to regain my composure. Did he really just say he was going to look for me on the plane? What had changed his mind? The plane wasn't huge, but it was packed, and with almost two hundred people on board, I suppose he still could've passed me by if he had decided to look. Judging by what he was wearing yesterday, and the way he's dressed today, he was probably in business class. I was in economy.

'I know Maria and Gunter. And Otto and Marielle, of course.'

'You do?'

He nods but he doesn't add how he knows them. He's not German, I'm certain of that. He sounds British to me, or maybe American. There's a hint of an accent but I can't place it and his voice is rich and smooth and deep and warm. It matches him to perfection. He's even more handsome than the first time we met.

And he was going to look for me on the plane!

And yet ... he didn't.

'Are you here on holiday?' he queries.

'Not really. I'm a–' I almost let it slip. I give a little cough, smile and continue. 'I'm a seasonaire. Or at least I'm trying to be. This is my first time and it's only a temporary job at Chalet Maria, via a friend of a friend.' I don't tell him it's via a friend of my brother.

'How temporary?'

'Erm. I guess we'll have to wait and see.' I laugh nervously.

'I'm sure you'll be great. Oh. I'm Rick, by the way. Did you say your name is Meg?'

'Uh-huh. And these are ... Ares and Beau, I think you called them.' I glance at the dogs who both look up at the mention of their names. They're covered from head to paw in snow and they shake themselves in unison sending showers of crumpled snowflakes everywhere. 'They're adorable!'

He laughs. 'They're like naughty toddlers. But yes, they're also adorable. Most of the time.'

'How long have you had them?'

He looks surprised. 'They're not mine. They're ...' he frowns. 'They belong to a friend of mine. He's ... busy today so I'm dog-sitting.'

'Does your friend live here?'

He clears his throat. He's trying to hide something and I don't know what or why but I can tell he is. And I should know because I'm hiding something too. He runs a hand through his thick, brown hair and darts a furtive glance back the way he came.

'He's ... staying here for a while.'

I can see Schloss Schatten through the trees.

'At Schloss Schatten?' I ask.

He meets my eyes and seems to search mine before he finally nods. 'A few of us are staying there.'

'I've heard it's where the rich and famous stay. Are you or your friend rich or famous?' I laugh as if it's a joke but he isn't amused.

'It's not only for rich and famous people. It's just a place to stay.'

'Of course. I expect everywhere here costs an arm and a leg at this time of year. Luckily for me, I get bed and board for free. I even get a lift pass. Except I don't ski. Although Otto has threatened to teach me.'

I'm trying to make light of it so I laugh again, and he's instantly more relaxed. I can see the frown lines dissipate, and the tension eases around his jaw.

'*Threatened* to teach you?' There's a hint of laughter in his voice too.

'Yeah. I foolishly watched some videos on YouTube of skiing accidents, before I came here. I have a feeling it may be more of a punishment than a treat. Broken bones are not on my wish list.'

'You should ask my … hosts about that. The owners of Schloss Schatten can tell you some horror stories.' He was going to say someone else. I'm sure of it. His friend, maybe?

'Thanks. But I'll give that a miss.'

He grins. 'That's probably wise.'

Ares and Beau trot over and sit down either side of him and suddenly I remember – I have seen those dogs before.

Not in the flesh but in a photo.

A photo of Cody Clayton. Lucinda Revere's fiancé.

Eleven

This man isn't Cody Clayton.

I've seen photos of Cody, and this isn't him.

Besides, he said his name is Rick.

But I've said I'm a seasonaire, and that's not true. Although ... in a way it is.

Truth is a funny thing. A half truth is still the truth. But is it also a lie? Yet, if the lies we tell are for good reasons, does that make them wrong? I've told people I like their new haircuts, or their new clothes, or their new partners, when in reality, I don't. Does that make me a bad person for telling lies? Or a good person for not wanting to hurt people's feelings?

And where do we draw the line? Is that when our lies are for selfish reasons?

I'm telling half truths to get the inside scoop on Lucinda and Cody's wedding. Photos of the bride and groom will bring joy to their millions of fans; it'll also help my career. And will it do any real harm to the happy couple?

Plus, if I don't do this, someone else will. Someone else might be here already, lens poised for the perfect shot.

Is that what Rick's doing here? He's definitely hiding something. I've just noticed the bag thrown over his shoulder looks very much like it might contain a camera. It's a similar bag to mine, only Rick's bag looks more expensive.

But that can't be the case if he's staying at Schloss Schatten and he's walking Cody's dogs.

Is he Cody's friend? He said he's here with some friends. Perhaps he's also friends with Lucinda.

Wouldn't that be something?

I may be wrong – and I usually am when it comes to matters of the heart – but I get the impression Rick might be attracted to me. I'm definitely attracted to him.

But I'm also attracted to Otto.

Which is irrelevant right now.

No wonder my head is spinning.

I need to get a grip.

'Meg?' Rick's now looking at me as if he's waiting for an answer.

'Sorry. What? I was miles away just then.'

Concern and doubt cloud his bright blue eyes, which are not as piercingly blue as Otto's; they're a softer, warmer blue, like a summer sky.

'I asked where you were going.' His gaze takes in my camera bag and I can tell from his expression, he's having doubts about me.

'Oh. To visit Ritterherzburg. I hear it's just as beautiful inside as it looks on the outside. And ancient. I must confess, I'd also like to get a look at the place you're staying. I'm told it's pretty special. I want to take some photos of the breathtaking scenery too. May I take a photo of your friend's dogs? My brother has a dog. He'd love to see these two.'

'I'd rather you didn't,' Rick says. 'They're a little camera-shy.'

I don't believe that for a second but I smile and nod my head.

'That's a pity, especially as they're so handsome. Lots of people must want to pet them and take photos. But I understand completely.'

'Do you?' His expression looks doubtful.

'I do.'

'That's good.'

An awkward silence now hangs between us, yet neither of us moves on. We smile at one another and he opens his mouth to speak but a shrill voice interrupts him.

'Ricky! R-icky!'

He closes his eyes for a second as if he's trying to shut it out but I peer along the footpath in the direction from which the voice is coming. The direction of Schloss Schatten.

She appears from the trees like a forest goddess, her long red hair flowing from beneath a dark green, faux fur, pillbox hat. Her hair cascades over her shoulders and the matching faux fur, standing collar of her dark green, full-length, poncho style cloak. The cloak has two rows of military style buttons, as far down as her waist, and from there it flaps open as she walks, revealing skin-tight, dark green trousers and black patent, thigh high boots. Her gloves are black as is the designer handbag swinging from one bent arm as she gingerly makes her way towards us.

Who in their right mind would wear boots like that in the snow? She should be on a catwalk somewhere.

I truly wish she were as she closes the gap between us. It's the stunning redhead from the airport.

'I can explain,' Rick says to me, his tone betraying his agitation.

'No explanation necessary,' I reply, hoping my tone isn't betraying my disappointment. I raise my hand in the air as nonchalantly as I can and I force a smile. 'It's been lovely chatting but I really must go. I need to be back in time to do my job.'

'Ricky!' The redhead sounds petulant as she glares at me and avoids the dogs. 'Why didn't you wait for me?'

Now I understand why he didn't look for me on the plane.

Ricky was otherwise engaged.

For a second time, I walk away, giving the redhead the briefest smile as I pass her.

And for a second time, he lets me.

Twelve

I'm letting my emotions get in the way of me doing my job, and as I stomp towards the castle, passing the path leading to Schloss Schatten and its formal gardens without as much as a glance, I give myself a telling off.

If *Ricky* ... or Rick ... is a friend of Cody Clayton's I should be getting to know him, not walking away like a stroppy teenager with a crush.

So what if the man has a girlfriend? I'm not here to fall in love. I'm here to get an inside scoop. What better way to find out all the details of this secret, winter wedding than to ask a friend of the groom?

Next time I see him, I must remind myself of that.

Assuming there is a next time.

At least I know where he's staying. And there's a chance Lucinda and Cody are staying there too.

Would it seem odd if I visited Schloss Schatten on the pretext of saying hello again to Rick?

Of course it would.

I'll have to find some other excuse.

I step out from the umbrella of trees into the warmth of winter sunshine, and the magnificent castle of Ritterherzburg towers before me in the near distance. This morning the sun was behind the castle and one group of mountains; now it is in front of the castle as it follows its path towards the west where it will set behind more mountains.

I take out my camera and snap some photos. I also take some on my phone. I'll send those to Mum and Dad later, and to Aaron too.

I might also send one to Tori, to let her know I'm here. We had a quick chat on Christmas Day, via Katie's phone, and I told her about my plan. She wasn't at all surprised and she didn't seem to mind. In fact, she sounded excited.

'I admire you for chasing your dream,' she said. 'I hope you get what you want. I can't wait to find out how it goes. Just try to avoid letting anyone know it was me who told you about it, if you can. Especially if you meet my boss.'

'Your secret's safe with me,' I said.

I appreciated the irony. I was getting a shot at my dream because Tori had given away someone else's secret.

I walk towards the castle and the windows appear to blink as sunlight hits them at various angles. The gleaming black, pointed roofs of the six turrets are spattered with melting snow and I notice one bears a star-like cross. It's almost identical in shape to the pictures I've seen of the golden cross on the summit of Zugspitze mountain, but this one is black instead of gold.

I'm not actually sure what either one is made of; iron, I suppose. Or bronze. I'll have to check on the internet. Not that it really matters. Both of them look beautiful. And it's not a travel piece I'm writing, so will anyone really care, apart from me?

I half expect a knight in shining black armour to come riding by on a sleek white horse, but instead a group of Japanese tourists bundle past me on the wide path leading to the entrance archway.

Several black birds circle above the castle, and a twinge of guilt runs through me. They're like feathered paparazzi with a bird's view. They resemble ravens or crows and as a group of six swoop down to the ground before me, I shiver unintentionally. But now I see they are smaller as they peck at the snow with their yellow beaks and strut around on long red legs. One watches me with its black beady eyes.

'They're Alpine coughs,' someone remarks.

I quickly turn, startled by the voice as it's so close. But the man isn't speaking to me. He's talking to the woman he's got his arm around, who is taking photos of the birds with her phone camera.

The couple smile at me and continue on their way. I take some photos of the birds and follow a little way behind. I seem to be the only tourist on my own, but it doesn't bother me. I remind myself again that I'm here to do a job.

Having purchased a ticket from the outer gate house, I join the next guided tour consisting of the couple I'd just seen, and four other tourists, together with the group from Japan.

We learn the original castle was built in 1220 which means it's been here for over eight hundred years and held by the same family, but it has been added to over the years.

We follow the guide into a room which is now an armoury. It has a stone floor, a massive arched fireplace, two small leaded light windows, and heavy wooden beams on the ceiling. The walls display bows, arrows, swords, shields, muskets and halberds from across the centuries. There are rows of pikes and four jousting lances, one of which is broken, having been retrieved after a tournament, details about which we're told.

From this room we are led along a stone corridor to what was once the living room. It has whitewashed walls hung with ancient tapestries, large stone pillars, another massive fireplace, this one larger than the last, rich, dark wood floors and matching heavy ceiling beams. Together with a few pieces of antique furniture dotted around the walls, there's a long refectory type table in the centre surrounded by twelve uncomfortable looking wooden chairs.

Next, we visit a bed chamber with a carved, four poster bed. There are faded but still colourful murals painted on the walls, from the 15th century, apparently. Thick wooden pillars stand between the wood floor and ceiling and the leaded light windows allow narrow beams of sunlight to dance across the floor towards yet another massive open fireplace.

It must cost a small fortune to heat this castle these days, as the family still reside here, but I suppose every room has a fireplace like the ones we've seen, and there is a forest right outside the castle gates.

From here, we go into a much larger, longer room. This is The Knight's Hall and it has an original, heavy oak beamed ceiling, heraldic frieze and a tiled floor. Magnificent suits of armour line the walls as if they're guarding the place to this day. Sunshine filters through the rows of leaded light windows, some of which contain stained glass. There are stone window seats with plump, embroidered cushions and a huge open fireplace, tall enough and wide enough for all of us to gather in. Not that we do. The guide says this room dates from 1510 and was mainly used for festivities, but also for meetings to discuss more serious events.

Finally, we are taken to the chapel. This is the room I've been dying to see and I'm not disappointed. It's only large enough to accommodate two dozen or so people on simply carved wooden pews. The altar is the original stone, draped with embroidered silks from the 16th century but the three stained glass windows behind it are also original and date from when the castle was first built or shortly after.

I let my imagination wander, and whilst I can picture many a knight and lady plighting their troths in here, somehow, I just can't see Lucinda Revere and Cody Clayton exchanging vows at this altar.

The chapel is beautiful. And serene. At least it probably is when it's not packed with tourists, but it doesn't say Pop Superstar or Olympic downhill skier to me.

Perhaps that's its appeal. Maybe Lucinda and Cody want something simple.

But if that's the case, why have their wedding in a castle?

It doesn't make any sense at all.

The tour ends, having taken around thirty minutes, and I leave the castle via the gift shop, purchasing a couple of very mini knights in armour that contain some German sweets. These knights are made of plastic, unlike the real armour found in almost every room inside the castle. I'll give one knight to Aaron and one to my dad.

I take some more photos before returning to Chalet Maria via the footpath through the forest. I'll admit I cast a glance in the direction of Schloss Schatten when I pass. It's twilight now, and even darker in the forest, and the lights from the chalet give a warm and welcoming ambience. I'm tempted to find an excuse to pay the place a visit, but as enticing as it is, I don't.

I walk faster, reaching Chalet Maria a few minutes before 5 p.m., so there's time for me to change, and to send some photos of Ritterherzburg to Mum and Dad and Aaron.

I also send one to Tori, and I wish I'd bought one of those knights for her. We had joked about us both wanting to find our own knights in shining armour so I know she would be amused. I might nip back tomorrow and get her one.

Thirteen

Like last night at 7 p.m., there's enough food on the table at dinner to feed twice as many people, yet somehow, we manage to empty almost every plate.

'It is the mountain air,' Maria informs me, when I say I can't believe how much I've eaten since I arrived. 'It does wonders for the appetite.'

'I think it's also because the food is so delicious,' I reply. 'Especially the cakes. I think the bee sting cake I had today is my new favourite.'

I'm a little ashamed to say, less than two hours ago, I stuffed my face with a slice of Black Forest cake, which is similar to the Black Forest Gateaux I've had back home in Norman Landing, only more delicious, and a slice of bee sting cake. I won't try to pronounce its name in German but I will say it's like eating a slice of heaven. I'm not sure where the name comes from, because it doesn't sting at all – although it might when I get on the scales.

Bruno, the chef, told me as I was peeling carrots for dinner, that it's made from a yeasted dough like a brioche bread, so it's not a sponge cake, but it looks like one ... only flatter. It has either a whipped cream layer or is filled with crème pâtissière, a sort of creamy custard, like the one I had today. The top has a generous coating of flaked almonds and honey, making the cake gooey, crunchy and caramelised, all at the same time.

'That is also my favourite,' says Marielle. 'Why is it called a bee sting cake?'

'There are two versions of where the name originated,' Gunter says. 'One is that a bee was attracted to the sweet honey topping and stung the baker who invented the cake. The other is that, in the 15th century, a group of bakers threw beehives at raiders from a neighbouring village, and once the raiders had retreated, the bakers made the cake in celebration.'

'I think I prefer the first version,' I say.

'I prefer the second,' says Otto, smiling at me as we begin to clear the table. 'Did you have a good day?'

He was almost late for dinner this evening, so he hasn't heard about my visit to the castle, but I've already told the others so, I don't want to repeat it all again.

'Yes, thanks. And you?'

He shrugs. 'It was good. But there are some people who are not meant to learn to ski, I have discovered, and today, I had two in my class. I believe I am a patient man, but sometimes...' He lets out a sigh and shakes his head.

'Not another accident?' I ask.

'No, no. I am glad to say. I did, however, tell those people not to return to me tomorrow, or there might be.' He grins wickedly. 'But it will not be an accident.'

'Otto!' I laugh. 'I definitely won't be coming to one of your classes then. You'll want to kill me after ten minutes.'

'Kill you?' Now the grin turns into a different kind of wicked and his eyes sparkle with devilment. He moves a little closer and waits a moment until we're alone in the room. 'Not kill you, no, Meg. Never.' He reaches out and touches a lock of my hair. 'But ... perhaps ... something else...'

He's gorgeous. There's no denying that. And it's been a very long time since I last had sex, but I quickly take a step away and laugh as if I think he's joking. Perhaps he is. I don't know. But I've seen that look before and it usually only leads to one thing. I don't have time for that.

'I should be so lucky,' I say. 'Which reminds me. Do you know a man named

Rick? He's a little taller than you. Dark hair, blue eyes, a lovely smile, casual but expensive clothes. He's staying at Schloss Schatten, I believe.'

Otto is watching me intently as I speak and although the grin is fading, it's still there.

He doesn't answer right away, so perhaps he's trying to remember but suddenly, he shakes his head and laughs.

'Yes. I know Rick. We are friends. Are we also competitors for your heart?'

I wave my free hand dismissively in the air, trying not to drop the plates I'm holding in the other, and laugh, but it sounds slightly maniacal to me.

'I don't think so. Besides, he's got a girlfriend. A stunning redhead with a body to die for.'

'Ah. That is Celestine.'

'Celestine?' I dislike her even more.

Otto's blond brows draw together. 'But she is not his girlfriend. Rick does not have a girlfriend and does not want one. He does not like ... to be tied down.' The wicked grin is back. 'Where as I like that very much.'

I don't think Otto's talking about girlfriends, but I need to know more about Rick.

'They looked as if they were in a relationship today. She told him off for not waiting for her.'

He stiffens noticeably. 'Today? I did not know that Celestine is here. She was with Rick, today?'

'Yes. That's why I thought they were a couple. I saw them at Heathrow airport yesterday too. They were on the same flight as me. At least he was and I think she must've been. I saw him again today on the footpath through the forest, near Schloss Schatten. He was walking his friend's dogs, Ares and Blue and Celestine came running after him.'

Otto's still tense. 'I thought you had seen them together in a photograph, perhaps. Not that she is here. But that is Celestine. She expects everyone to wait for her. To do her bidding. She is not pleased when they do not.'

He sounds as though he's speaking from experience. The flirting stops and he walks towards the kitchen with the tray he's filled with cups and glasses.

'Otto? Do you know who owns the dogs? They're gorgeous Huskies and I'd like to take some photos of them.'

'Yes,' he says. 'They belong to Cody. He is a friend of Rick's. And also of mine. But Cody does not like people to take photos. He is ... shy of cameras.'

'Cody? You don't mean Cody Clayton? The Olympic downhill skier. He must have his photo taken all the time.'

'Yes. When he competes, that is fine, but when he is not, he does not like it.' Otto stops and briefly turns to face me. 'Do you know Cody, also?'

'No. I've just seen him in photos on the internet. There're quite a lot. There's even one of him with the dogs, so he can't be that camera-shy.'

'That would have been taken by Rick. Most of the photos you will see of Cody in his private life, are Rick's.'

'Rick is a photographer?'

'Yes. A winter sports photographer.' Otto gives me a curious look. 'You do not know much about him?'

'No. But I'd like to.'

He shakes his head and shrugs. 'Be careful what you wish for. That is what you say, is it not? I like Rick very much, but I will warn you. Rick will break your heart.'

'He won't. Because I won't let him. I'm not here to fall in love.'

'It is not always our choice.' Otto shoves open the kitchen door with his hip and holds it open for me to pass. The others are in the kitchen loading the dishwasher and getting ready to serve dinner to the guests. 'I will tell you one more thing about him. He was also World Champion, twice, but an accident ended his skiing career some years ago. He does not like to talk of it, so it is better if you do not ask.’

Fourteen

I can't stop thinking about what Otto told me concerning Rick.

It was on my mind the entire evening; all the while Marielle and I were serving dinner to the guests, and after that, when we were clearing the tables, and again when I went to bed at 10.30 p.m. – which is considered early for a seasonaire – on the pretext of wanting to finish a book I said I was reading.

Worst of all, I even dreamt about Rick's accident last night. I saw him skiing down a mountain at breakneck speed, crashing into the bright red safety netting and landing in a crumpled heap. I woke up calling his name, and afterwards, I couldn't get back to sleep.

I only have myself to blame. I didn't know Rick's surname but I searched the internet via my phone, for 'downhill skier Rick and skiing accident', on the assumption that there couldn't be many downhill skiers named Rick who were involved in skiing accidents. The list of search results, surprisingly, found two Ricks, but most of the results were for Rick Price and, after reading the details and studying the images, it was clear that it was him. And then I foolishly watched videos of the accident on YouTube.

It made Cody's accident seem like the equivalent of a grazed knee. Unlike Cody, Rick did not get up and walk away from his. He was strapped onto a stretcher and airlifted to hospital by the rescue helicopter. He underwent a nine-hour surgery for a broken tibia and fibula in each leg, plus a fractured hip, a broken wrist, a broken arm and two broken ribs. It was a miracle he didn't break his neck or spine.

There were several news reports of the story and his subsequent recovery and I read them all.

It was feared Rick would never walk again, let alone clip on a pair of skis, but it seems he was determined.

With a number of metal rods, pins and bolts holding his leg bones together, he spent two weeks in hospital followed by several months in a wheelchair and then almost two months on crutches.

He endured daily physical therapy, even though he must have been in excruciating pain.

Most of the rods, pins and bolts in both of his legs were eventually removed, but he was left with a permanent metal rod in his left leg.

It took him over a year to recover and he never returned to competitive skiing. He took up winter sports photography instead.

There were a few articles on that, and thousands of his photographs, many of which were of Cody and his fellow teammates, skiing.

I didn't look at them all, obviously – that would've taken all night. Probably longer. But the ones I did see were excellent and, somewhat depressingly, made me feel a little inadequate. Rick definitely has an eye for the perfect shot.

He was twenty-nine when the accident happened six years ago, making him thirty-five at present, and, having won the World Cup for two years running, he was on track to win his third. After Rick's accident, Cody won that year, and Cody's won it twice since then, including last year, plus an Olympic Gold medal.

I also discovered that Rick's an only child and that his parents and close friends helped him through his recovery. At the time of his accident, he had a long term girlfriend, so in spite of what Otto said, Rick wasn't always anti-girlfriends. One report said they broke up after the accident; the others didn't mention her. There was no mention of a girlfriend since, but there were a lot of photos of him with beautiful women, one of whom I recognised as Celestine.

So although I'm up early this morning, I feel like death warmed over as I stare out of the family dining room window into the twilight. I probably look like it too. It's just gone 6.30 a.m. and I'm on my third cup of coffee. It's going to be one of those days.

I've got to get my act together. Today is the 29th which means the secret winter wedding is in three days, counting today and the wedding day, so it's more like two and a half really, and I'm no closer to getting this scoop now than I was when I got on the plane.

That's not strictly true. I now know two people who are friends with the groom-to-be. If I play my cards right surely one of them can get me an introduction to the man himself.

'Good morning,' Otto says, as he shoves open the kitchen door and I turn to see who it is. 'You are up with the lark. That is the English saying, is it not?'

'Good morning. Yes it is. But this lark is very sleepy.'

Otto joins me at the window, hugging a large mug of coffee. He looks a bit like I feel, but that's because he went out last night and didn't get home until 3 a.m., which I know, as I was wide awake and I heard him. His bedroom is opposite mine and although he was probably being as quiet as he could be, the doors in this place squeak.

'This lark also.' He grins at me.

'Do you have many classes today?'

He nods as he gulps his coffee. 'The day is full, but there will be sunshine and I will sleep in the sun at lunchtime, at the top of Zugspitze.' He stares out into the semi-darkness as if he's picturing the moment right now.

Zugspitze and the other mountains are visible in the near-distance and I'm tempted to ask if I can join him. I'd like to see the golden cross at the summit and I've read that there's a restaurant up there too. The views must be spectacular. But if he wants to sleep at lunchtime, my presence might make him feel he can't, so perhaps I'll venture up there by myself. Luckily, I can take the cable car or the cogwheel train so there won't be any need for me to have a crash-course in skiing.

Oh dear. Crash-course now has me thinking about Rick Price yet again. I need to put a stop to that.

'I saw Rick and Celestine last night,' says Otto.

So much for me *not* thinking about Rick.

And now I'm also jealous of the stunning redhead. What on earth is wrong with me?

I look directly at Otto but he seems to be avoiding eye contact and even in profile, there's an odd expression on his face, almost as if he doesn't want to think about them either but, like me, he just can't help himself.

'Really? Where was that?'

'At the Irish Pub. It is a popular venue for seasonaires. You should have come out with me last night. You would have enjoyed it. I saw them again later, at a nightclub. I do not recall which one as my friends and I visited several. The nightlife here is good with many such places.'

'Maybe next time,' I say, also wishing I had gone with him.

'Rick mentioned you.'

Now he turns his head and looks me directly in the eye as I suck in a surprised breath and stare at him, open-mouthed.

'He did?'

'Yes. He asked me if you were out. I told him you were at home in bed, reading a book you wanted to finish.'

Oh great! Now the man will think I'm boring. Not that there is anything boring about reading a book, but I've read that seasonaires have a reputation for partying the night away, not for being tucked up in bed by 10.30 – unless it's with a man … or a woman. Basically, unless it's for sex. For a book? No.

'What did he say about that?' I ask tentatively.

Otto looks away and shakes his head. 'Nothing.'

Oh joy. The man wasn't even surprised. Or perhaps he didn't care.

But why had he asked in the first place?

'Good morning!' Marielle breezes in, looking beautiful. 'Did you finish your book?'

'My book? Oh yes. My book. I did.'

'You did not sleep well?'

Her tone suggests it's a question, but her expression tells me it's one to which she already knows the answer. I obviously do look as bad as I feel. I should've put on some make-up.

'Not particularly.'

'The bed is uncomfortable?'

'No! It's wonderful. I think I've simply got too much on my mind.'

Otto darts a sideways glance at me as if he knows precisely what that is, but he drinks his coffee and pulls his beeping phone from the pocket of his jeans. A smile curves on his lips as he taps out a reply and he slowly turns to face me, but he doesn't say a word.

'You should take some mountain air today,' Marielle says. It sounds more like a command than a suggestion. 'It will clear your mind and your lungs and will make your heart sing.'

My mind could do with clearing but I think my lungs are fine and as for my heart singing, well, it'll take more than mountain air to do that.

'Maybe I will,' I say, without the slightest intention of doing so.

'We do not serve dinner tonight,' Marielle says. 'Today we will relax after breakfast and our work. Mama and I can manage if you would like to explore.'

Marielle told me the day I arrived that one evening each week the guests fend for themselves and eat out at any of the selection of restaurants in town.

'That's very kind, but I've hardly done a thing since I arrived. I am supposed to be helping.'

'You have,' she says, laughing. 'You are. You can help with breakfast this morning, and some cleaning, and then the day is yours.'

She turns and heads back to the kitchen so there's no chance for me to argue the point, and when I look at Otto to gauge his opinion, he simply shrugs and smiles.

It's odd that no one has asked me anything about the story I am supposed to be here to write. I wonder if my brother has let the cat out of the bag and told Hugh all about it, and in turn, Hugh has told Greta, who has told her family.

Yet, surely if they knew, they would mention it, wouldn't they? Especially bearing in mind Cody is a friend of Otto's.

Perhaps they simply respect other people's privacy and assume I'll tell them about it if I want to share.

That sends an arrow of guilt straight to my heart. They are all such lovely, kind and generous people and I suddenly feel as if I'm betraying them in some way.

But this story could change my life. It could definitely change my career. Do I really want to spend my future writing tongue-in-cheek advice columns and local news articles, and taking a few photos for a newspaper with a circulation of no more than a couple of thousand at best. The astonishing success of the Saving Christmas campaign did boost the numbers, but it remains to be seen if any of those increases stick.

The most popular bridal magazines each have a distribution of something in the region of forty to fifty thousand. Numbers have dropped considerably now that many people read on line, but digital sales have doubled over the last year and are expected to continue to rise. My work could reach thousands, or possibly hundreds of thousands, not just the population of Norman Landing.

Best of all, it should mean that I could earn more money, and that would enable me to finally be able to travel more, and to really see the World.

Don't get me wrong, I love living in Norman Landing. I love being so close to my family and friends. I love living by the sea. It's just that there's a big wide world out there and it's all waiting to be seen.

The guests all eat breakfast early, apart from the two women staying in the 'messy' room, as I've come to call it – the one with all the cosmetics on the shelves, and almost everyone has left by 8 a.m. or shortly after. Most of the ski lifts open at 8.30 a.m. and it amazes me how eager the guests are to queue to get on the slopes. Again, apart from the messy room women. They don't leave until 8.45 a.m. and they don't appear to be in much of a hurry even then.

I start cleaning as soon as the first room is clear and now that I seem to have a routine, I make swift progress. I thought it would take me ages to get the hang of being a seasonaire but I already feel as if I'm an old hand and I've only been doing the job for two days.

There's more to it than just cleaning, of course, but I haven't really been involved in that much else. I have helped out in the kitchen, assisted with some baking and prepped a few hundred vegetables. I've served the guests and cleared the tables, loaded the dishwasher and emptied it, but I haven't done any ordering of supplies or shopping. I haven't booked guests in and out. Or arranged trips to nearby beauty spots and other destinations either. Which is probably just as well, as I don't know where they are.

By 9.30 a.m. I've finished and I head to my room to get washed and changed. Now I do put on a touch of make-up but only mascara and lipstick. I take my hair out of its ponytail, brush out some tangles and let it hang loose.

The sun may be shining but I know from yesterday it's going to be cold outside, so I put on my bright red cowl and matching scarf and slip my red matching gloves into my camera bag. I go downstairs and take my fawn, padded coat from the cloakroom and pull on my fur-lined boots.

Otto left at 8.a.m. and I said goodbye to him, so the people laughing in the sitting room must be Maria, Marielle and Gunter. I pop my head around the door to wish them a relaxing day, but the words stick in my throat.

It isn't just the three of them who are sitting on the plump sofas in front of the fire, drinking coffee and laughing and chatting happily. Rick Price is also there.

Fifteen

'Hello again,' Rick says, almost as if we're friends, and smiles at me like we are. 'I came to see Otto but he'd already left, so I'm spending time with Maria, Marielle and Gunter instead.'

'That's nice,' I say, inwardly cringing at how pleased I am to see him. 'I'm on my way out, so I just popped in to say goodbye and have a lovely day.' I smile at everyone except Rick.

'You are going to Zugspitze?' Marielle asks, and although it is a question, it still sounds more like a command.

'Erm. I haven't decided yet.'

'The mountain air will put colour in your cheeks,' says Gunter, making me wish I'd applied some blusher.

'Perhaps Rick would accompany you,' Maria suggests, smiling first at me and then at Rick.

'Oh, no!' I say, a little too quickly.

'I'd love to,' says Rick, at the same time.

'You do not speak German,' Marielle reminds me.

'Will I need to? Everyone I've met so far seems to speak English very well.'

'Not everyone.' Gunter winks at me, but I'm not sure why.

'I speak German,' Rick informs me.

I'm not in the least bit surprised.

'I couldn't possibly ask you to come with me and I don't want to be a nuisance. Besides, I'm sure you've got plans.'

'No. I'm as free as a bird.'

'So Otto tells me.'

Whoops! I hadn't meant to say that out loud.

Rick quirks one eyebrow and gives me a curious look.

'It is settled,' Maria says, pouring herself more coffee from the pot on the table beside her.

I want to think of something to say to get out of this awkward situation, but I can't think of a thing.

'You will feel much better once you are at the top,' says Marielle.

'Are you unwell?' Rick actually looks concerned and takes a step towards me.

'No. I'm fine. Just tired. I didn't get much sleep last night.'

'The bed is uncomfortable?' Maria is even more concerned than Rick.

'The bed is wonderful. It was just one of those nights.'

Rick comes over and stands close beside me. 'Good book?' he whispers.

I'd like to wipe that smile right off his face.

'Honestly,' I say, adding a slight hiss to my tone. 'I'm very happy to go alone.'

'And I'm very happy to go with you.'

'But you must have stuff to do!'

'Must I? Like what?'

'Like ... taking your friend's dogs for a walk.'

He opens the door wider and indicates with his extended hand that I should exit before him.

'I did that earlier,' he says and then smiles at the others. 'Have a great day. See you later.'

'Enjoy yourselves,' says Maria, as Marielle and Gunter both give us a little wave.

Clearly I have no choice.

'Bye then,' I say, raising one hand to wave back. 'Have fun.'

Rick retrieves his all-weather jacket from the cloakroom, slips his socked-feet into his boots and ties the laces, and then looks up and beams at me.

'I think this is going to be fun,' he says.

I think it's going to be awkward, but I don't say that.

Then again, it does provide me with the perfect opportunity to find out all I can about Cody and Lucinda and their secret winter wedding, so I must look on the bright side.

Besides, didn't I want to get to know Rick better? Spending some time with him on a mountain is as good a place as any to start.

'If we're taking a trip up Zugspitze,' he says, as we leave the chalet and walk towards the town via a footpath in the snow, 'we should do the round trip. It takes in all the must-see views. The golden cross on the summit, the mountain railway and cable cars, spectacular views of Lake Eibsee, stunning vistas of four countries and more than four hundred mountain peaks. Oh, and a couple of restaurants too.'

'What's not to like?'

He grins at me. 'It'll take about three hours or so, depending on how long we stop and admire the views, or eat cake and drink coffee.'

'We'll need at least forty minutes for that. Each stop.'

He laughs, and it's a sound I like, especially when he says, 'If we add lunch, we could be out all day.'

'I don't have to work tonight, so it's not a problem for me.'

His brows knit together for a second as he looks at me and there's something about his expression that I can't quite fathom.

'It's not for me either. But I have a feeling it could be.' He coughs and continues, 'We'll start at the Zugspitzebahn and take the cogwheel train via the valley and the tunnel up to the Zugspitze Plateau. It's possible to go hiking, tobogganing, or take a tour of the glacier from there, if you'd like to. We can stop for coffee and cake in the Sonnalpin. It's a Bavarian style restaurant which is right by the glacier and it has fantastic views.'

'Sounds great so far. I'd love to get some shots of the glacier. I'm not sure I've ever seen one before. Not in real life, at least. Just on the TV.' I tap my camera bag. 'I've got my camera with me.'

He tuts. 'I should've brought mine. I'll have to make do with my phone.'

'We could go back and get it,' I suggest. It might be a chance for me to get inside Schloss Schatten and to see if Cody and Lucinda are there.

He smiles and shakes his head. 'No. It won't kill me to be without it for one day. I've been here quite a few times so I've got plenty of photos of the place already.'

'Every day is different in front of a camera lens.'

'That's true. But I can always ask for copies of yours. The train and cable cars will be busy as it's the holiday season and standing in a queue for hours is not the best way to spend our time.'

'Okay. So after coffee and cake at the Sonnalpin, where do we go next?'

'The Gletscherbahn cable car will take us to the top station and from there it's only a few metres to the golden cross at the summit. The summit station is glass, and the restaurant, Panorama 2962, is almost three thousand metres above sea level, as its name suggests, so you get truly sensational views of Germany, Austria, Italy and Switzerland. The restaurant also serves delicious meals, so I think that's where we should have lunch.'

'Even though we'll have just had cake? Forget that. What am I saying? Since I've been here I've eaten four times as much as usual. I'll be ready for lunch within an hour of the cake.'

He laughs again. 'That's the mountain air. It gives you an appetite. We'll have a leisurely lunch, and if the sun stays out, which it is supposed to according to the forecast, we can sit and soak up some rays. After that, we'll take the ultramodern Zugspitze cable car. Some people find the journey a little frightening, mainly because of the height. It's a difference of two kilometres between the mountain stations and the valley below.'

'How much!' I shriek. 'I'm not sure I like the sound of that. I'm not a huge fan of heights, especially not if I'm in a tin can on a rope.'

He grins at me. 'And you're going to the summit of a mountain, why?'

'Because I like to face my fears. And I want to see the world. I'm just not sure about the tin can.'

'It's hardly a tin can, and it is a world record holder. Three world records. The first is, its steel supports are the highest of their kind. Next is, the difference in altitude, as I've mentioned, and the third is, it has the longest span of freely suspended wire rope at a little over three kilometres between two sections.'

'You're not selling me on it with those facts. "Freely suspended wire rope" sounds particularly stomach churning.'

'You'll be fine. I'll hold your hand if you're scared.'

'You'll hold my hand! And that'll save me from falling to a certain death, will it?'

I am trying to play it cool but the thought of holding his hand sends a tingly feeling shooting through me. Even if I'm not scared, I might pretend to be.

'I promise you won't fall. It's completely safe. Oh, and you'll have breathtaking views of Lake Eibsee throughout the journey down, which only takes about fifteen minutes. We can go for a stroll by the lake if you like. The wraparound path of the Eibsee Circuit Trail takes over two hours, so we won't do that today.'

'After being in a tin can two kilometres above the valley floor, I may not be able to walk at all. My legs might've turned to jelly. Erm. Is that a Christmas market? It's a bit late, isn't it?'

I point at a stall containing a Nativity scene, nestled amongst a row of six or seven stalls in front of a beautiful old church. The aromas wafting towards me are divine. I'd been so engrossed in our conversation that I hadn't noticed where we are.

'Yes. In Germany, the holidays continue up to and including Epiphany, which is on January 6th, and there are still some Christmas markets until then. They're smaller than the pre-Christmas ones and the stalls tend to sell mainly mulled wine, punch, and bratwurst, plus a few local craft items.'

'I like the sound of mulled wine. It's a bit early though.'

'It's always too early for mulled wine, as far as I'm concerned.'

'More of a beer-man, are we?'

'More of a whisky-man, in truth. But beer is good on a night out.' He gives me that odd look again. 'I thought you might be out last night.'

'Nope. But I hear you were out with Celestine.'

'I wasn't *with* her.' He takes a breath, lets it out and runs a hand through his hair. 'Sorry. I didn't mean to snap. I was out and so was she, but we weren't together. Not in the sense I think you mean. I'm not dating her.'

'Message received, loud and clear.' I smile. 'And it's none of my business anyway. But why did it annoy you so much?'

He shakes his head. 'Celestine has a way of ... well, let's just say, I don't like people getting the wrong impression, and leave it at that.'

It doesn't really explain why he was annoyed but I don't want to push it. We're getting on really well and I want to keep it that way.

'I love all the frescoes on the buildings. Would you mind if I stop to take a photo?' It's a particularly beautiful one of a mountain scene with goats and a goatherd wandering across a summer meadow.

'Of course not. Let me hold your bag.' He reaches out and takes it and I rummage around inside to get my camera.

'Do the meadows really look like that in summer? Or have you only been here in winter?'

'What makes you think that?' There's a slight furrow between his dark brows.

'Erm.' I shrug nonchalantly. The man is super-sensitive to my every word. He's definitely hiding something. 'You just seem like a winter sort of guy.'

Now he raises his brows. 'I'm not sure what that means, but I'll take it as a compliment. And yes. The meadows do look like that in summer. They're also beautiful in spring and autumn.'

I take a few shots of the fresco and say, 'So you come here year-round? You must really like the place.'

'I do. I love it here. It's not the highest ski town in the world and sometimes the snow conditions aren't great, and it's packed at this time of year, but there's something about this place that makes us feel ... me feel, as if I'm home.'

'You said "us". Is there something you're not telling me? Like a wife and five kids back at the chalet.'

'No! No wife. No kids.'

I know he's not married but he did say "us" and I want to know who that is, so this time I will push it. I put my camera back and I'm about to take my bag from him but he swings it onto his shoulder and starts to move on.

'You and Celestine?'

He stops, turns and glares at me for a nano-second and then he smiles. 'Definitely not. Okay. I was referring to a friend. My best friend.'

'Ah. The owner of the dogs. Can he not be mentioned by name? Please don't tell me he's the King of Spain or something and you're really his bodyguard.'

His grin is devastatingly gorgeous.

'Close. But not quite.' He holds my gaze for a moment as if he's wondering whether to say something more. 'His name is Cody. Cody Clayton.'

I can tell he's expecting me to react to that so I pretend the name means nothing to me.

'That sounds like he's American. The name rings a bell. I think he's a friend of Otto's too.'

His brows shoot up. 'Seriously? You haven't heard of Cody Clayton?'

Now I'm going to have to lie and I'd rather not do that to him, so I compromise.

'What? Am I being dim? Is he famous or something?'

Rick shakes his head and laughs. 'You're obviously not a ski-groupie.'

'Erm. Is that a compliment? Or not? What is a ski-groupie when it's at home?'

He looks a little bemused.

'They're people who follow famous skiers around and ... try to spend time with them, to put it politely. You do know that GaPa is one of the venues for heats in The Alpine Ski World Cup, don't you? And that the annual New Year's Ski Jump, which is part of the Four Hills Tournament takes place on January 1st at the Olympic Ski Jump here?'

'If I didn't before, I do now.'

'You're really not into skiing at all, are you?'

'Not really. We don't get much snow in Norman Landing. That's the seaside town I come from. It's more of a big village than a town. It's on the south-east coast of England. We did get snow this year, as it happens. Quite a lot of it. But it's a rarity.'

'So why did you want to be a seasonaire? The pay's not great, although the tips can be. But seasonaire jobs mainly appeal to people who love to ski, or do some other winter sport.'

'Erm. Yeah. The truth is, I love taking photos. I would do that all day if I could. And I do love snow. I heard about this place from a friend and heard about the chalet via another friend of a friend. I had some time off and fancied a break so when I got the chance to stay at Chalet Maria for a few days, in exchange for helping out, I grabbed the chance with both hands. Being a seasonaire gives me plenty of free time to take photos in the snow.'

'I see. Well I can't argue with that. I'm a photographer too. It's what I do for a living. A winter sports photographer, mainly, but like you, I just love taking photos.'

'Wow! You're so lucky. I envy you.'

'Don't. You can do it too, if you want it badly enough. It's hard work, like any job and there are good days and bad, and lots of standing around, but it's worth it when you get that perfect shot. I love my job. Although I do take time off, which is why I haven't got my camera stuff today. There's more to life than work. I learnt that the hard way, a few years ago.'

'Oh I want it. Believe me. And I'll work my socks off to get it, if I can.' That sounded a bit obsessive so I add, 'But for now I'm happy just being here.'

'And I'm happy you came. So what do you do back in Norman Landing? Yesterday you said this is a temporary job, but it sounded as if it might become more than that.'

'Erm. Yeah.' I must stop saying, "erm". I need to think more quickly on my feet. 'I was involved in a campaign to help some old aged pensioners before Christmas and it opened my eyes to other possibilities. I'm at a bit of a crossroad in my life and I'm taking this time out to think about my future and to see where I can go from here. But tell me more about your friend Cody and The Alpine Ski World Cup and The Four Hills thingammy. From what you've said, I assume Cody is a famous skier and that groupies are a problem for him. Is he competing in the World Cup this year?'

I know he isn't competing this year because of his accident. I'd read that on the internet. I hadn't read anything about ski-groupies though.

It's as if a dark cloud has descended. The laughter fades in Rick's eyes and his mouth forms a hard line, as does his jaw. We walk on as I wait for him to respond and after a while he does.

'He's not competing. He had an accident at the end of November during an event at Lake Louise in Canada. He wasn't seriously hurt, thank God, just a fractured wrist, but ... due to other things going on, he pulled out of the championships. It's a bummer, because he probably would've won again this year and that would've made the announcement ... erm ... he's won the World Cup three times and this would've been his fourth. He's also an Olympic Gold medallist.'

Announcement. Rick definitely said "announcement". Are Lucinda and Cody planning to announce their secret winter wedding before they get hitched? Or after? Surely it must be after, otherwise it wouldn't be a secret wedding, would it? Not that it is a total secret, thanks to Tori.

'I'm glad he's okay. But he must be bitterly disappointed. Especially if he expected to win. A fractured wrist shouldn't put him out of action for too long, and there's always next year, isn't there?'

Rick looks torn. I'm sure he wants to tell me something, but he can't. He's probably been sworn to secrecy and, unlike Tori, it's a secret he is determined to keep.

That makes me like him more, even though it doesn't help me with my scoop.

'The queue's not bad,' he says, pointing a little ahead to where people are standing in line, many with skis or snowboards in their arms. Our departure station is close to the main station where I first arrived in GaPa. 'We should be on the train within twenty minutes.'

'I can't wait,' I say. 'I'm rather excited now.'

Surprisingly, that's not a lie. I am.

Sixteen

I honestly can't remember the last time I enjoyed myself as much as I am today.

The trip on the cogwheel train was slow but comfortable. I would have liked it more if Rick had sat beside me instead of opposite, but at least it meant I could look him directly in the eyes while we chatted during the fifty minutes or so journey. The scenery in the valley was beautiful with snow-covered houses and forests passed along the way. I could feel the air grow cooler as we began to climb the mountain and again, the views of the valley and also the lake that Rick had mentioned, Lake Eibsee, were sublime.

I lost count of the number of photos I took once we reached the plateau and I got to see my first glacier in real life. Rick was right about the cake and coffee at the Sonnalpin restaurant. It was a great place to stop. From there to the summit only took about five minutes but the views from the top truly took my breath away. I actually couldn't speak for at least a couple of minutes and Rick jokingly waived his hands in front of my face as if to wake me from a trance.

And yes, we did have a leisurely lunch at Panorama 2962, where it took me quite a while to decide what I would have. There were specialities from Germany, Austria, Italy and Switzerland. The restaurant has a motto which is: "the best from 4 countries", and I can confirm that's probably true. Not that I tried every dish on the menu, obviously.

'Why not have something from each country?' Rick suggested, grinning at me over his menu.

'Are you getting impatient? Or just trying to make me fat? How much weight does that tin can we are going in later, actually take?'

He burst out laughing. 'You've got a point. We may have to walk down.' He winked at me before placing his menu face down on the table. 'That was a joke by the way. And take your time. We've got all afternoon.'

I eventually decided on the crusty roasted pike-perch fillet with saffron and fennel Rick had a tender looking steak with a Gorgonzola sauce. For dessert, we shared a chocolate fondue with fresh fruit. Rick ordered a glass of white wine for me. It was a local, Bavarian wine and had a name I'd never heard of but it was crisp and refreshing and perfect with my fish.

'It's not mulled wine, is it?' I joked, when he ordered beer for himself.

'No.' He grinned at me. 'I do like the local wines, and I wanted you to try one, but I fancied a beer. Would you prefer a beer?'

'No thanks. I prefer wine.'

The weather was glorious and although it was cold, we sat in the sun after lunch, drinking coffee and admiring the spectacular views.

And, half an hour later, we are still sitting in the sunshine.

'Marielle was right,' I say, soaking up the rays bathing my face. 'I did need this and I do feel so much better. In fact, I feel as if I've died and gone to heaven.'

'I feel that too.'

My eyes are closed, but there is something in his tone that makes me open them and look at him, and when I do, it isn't just the sunshine that gives me an intensely warm glow.

We are sitting side-by-side on two chairs, which are a bit like the deckchairs on the beach at home, and for one unbelievable moment, I think he is going to lean across and kiss me.

'Hello!' Otto's cheery greeting breaks the magic between us and he comes to a swishing halt right in front of our chairs.

I'm far more disappointed than I should be; Rick looks both disappointed and embarrassed. Otto just looks pleased to see us.

'I am late,' Otto says, as if we are expecting him.

'For what?' I ask, looking from Otto to Rick.

Rick's face is flushed, even though he's tanned, and the crimson on his cheeks is not just from the sun.

'I have a confession to make,' he says. 'I texted Otto early this morning, to see if he was free.'

'I told him that my day was full, but that I could stop for a beer.'

'I was going to meet him here, for lunch.'

'I told him that you might like to join us because today is your day off.'

So I thought I might ask if you wanted to spend the morning with me. Only Maria suggested it for me.'

It's like watching a tennis match as they bat explanations between them. I remember Otto getting a text as we drank coffee, but that was before sunrise. Was that text from Rick?

Why do I get the feeling that they had this day planned out? I just can't figure out why.

'Let me see if I understand this,' I say, getting to my feet. 'When you came to Chalet Maria this morning, you already knew Otto wouldn't be there?'

Rick nods. 'Yes.'

'So you lied?'

'What? No.' He frowns and jumps to his feet and then looks contrite. 'Technically, yes, I suppose I did. But for a good reason.'

'What reason? Why couldn't you just ask me? Why did you need to pretend it was a spontaneous moment? And did you ask Maria to suggest it?'

'No.' He grins briefly. 'She did that of her own volition. But I was very glad she did.'

'Why? Were you too afraid to ask me out yourself?'

'Not afraid, exactly. No. But I knew this would happen.'

'Knew what would happen?'

'This. That you would think I was asking you out on a date, or something. And I'm not.'

'What! Now I'm totally confused.'

He lets out a quick sigh and shakes his head.

Otto shrugs and backs away. 'I need to get a beer. I will be back soon. Would either of you like anything?'

'Not me, thanks,' says Rick.

'No, thank you,' I say to Otto, and once he's gone I turn to Rick. 'But from you, I'd like an explanation.' I cross my arms and glower at him.

He takes a deep breath and looks me in the eye. 'I'm sure this sounds ridiculous to you, but I don't have girlfriends. I don't do relationships. I don't make long-term plans. I did that once. Never again.'

'Yes. So Otto tells me. What does that have to do with this?'

He raises both brows in surprise. 'Everything. I knew that, if I asked you to spend the morning with me, you would think it was a date. If I asked to see you again, you would think it was a second date. And then, if I asked to see you a third time, you would think you were my girlfriend.'

I can't help myself. I burst out laughing. 'Are you being serious, right now?'

He looks a little offended. 'Yes. Absolutely. Are you saying you wouldn't think those things?'

I ponder the matter for a second. 'I might. I think anyone would.'

'Exactly my point.'

'Okay, genius. But let me ask you this. Why would you ask me out ... Sorry. Ask to see me, more than once if you don't want a relationship? I realise there are people who hook up more than once, and sometimes often, just for sex and nothing else, but if that's the case, and that's what you want, you could have simply told me that, the moment we left the chalet. Or made that clear when you asked me out. Sorry. Asked to spend time with me.'

'And you'd have been fine with that?'

Now I shrug. 'Either I would, or I wouldn't, but at least we would have both known where we stood and you wouldn't have needed to go through this whole charade. To pretend you really like me and you're enjoying my company.'

'I'm not pretending. I do like you. I am enjoying your company.'

'But not enough for me to be your girlfriend? That's not a trick question. I'm simply aiming for clarity.'

He hesitates for the merest second. 'No.'

'Fine.'

'Erm ...' He looks like a little boy again, just as he did at Heathrow, as he flicks a lock of hair from his eyes. 'What happens now?'

'What would you like to happen now?'

'I ... I would like to spend the afternoon with you, as planned. And to see you again, if possible. But it's not just about what I want, is it?'

'No. It's not. I'm happy to spend the afternoon with you … as planned. If I enjoy it, I'm happy to see you again. And now that we both know exactly what's going on here – that you like me and I like you, we can cut to the chase, can't we?'

He brightens visibly. 'Can we? I thought we already had. Now I'm the one who doesn't understand. But I'm pleased you're not mad with me and that you're happy for us to spend more time together.'

'Bearing in mind I'm leaving on the 4th of January, were you hoping to go to bed with me at some stage in the near future? Or are you going to wait for Maria to suggest that too?'

Seventeen

No woman wants to be told by a man she's got a crush on that she isn't 'girlfriend material', and although I know it's not just me, it's every woman, as far as Rick's concerned, it doesn't make it any less hurtful.

But what did I expect? Love at first sight? Hearts and flowers? Declarations of his undying love?

Yeah right. Like any of that is ever going to happen to me.

Yet for a moment. No – for a few moments, since we met, I did actually think there might be something magical happening between me and Rick.

I told you I'm not good at this romance stuff.

At least I might be having sex with a handsome man in the very near future.

I can't help but laugh. He's just told me he was going to the loo, but I think he's gone to find Otto and to get his advice. Or at least, his opinion.

When I said the bit about us going to bed, his face was a picture. I wish I'd taken a photograph. It was a combination of shock, delight and fear. I've never seen that expression on a man's face before. It's almost worth having a broken heart for.

Not that I've got a broken heart.

I may be wrong about Rick. He might've just gone to the loo. Otto is returning with a beer in his hand – and a beautiful woman on his arm.

'Where is Rick?' he asks.

'The loo, I think.'

'The loo?' the woman queries, with a strong Italian accent.

'It is English for ... gabinetto,' Otto says.

I assume that must be toilet or loo in Italian, because the woman nods, says, 'Me also,' and sashays off towards the toilets. I'm not sure how she manages to walk so sexily in ski boots. I've been having trouble walking normally in mine.

'This is interesting,' I say, once she's out of earshot.

'The woman?' He shrugs and grins at me. 'A private lesson. Nothing more.'

'No, Otto. Not the woman. Rick, and the text this morning. Didn't you warn me that he would break my heart?'

'Did you not tell me he would not, because you will not let him?'

'I did. But is throwing us together wise?'

'That is for you and Rick to decide. I did not throw you together. Rick told me last night that he likes you. I told him that you like him. The text today was to ask if you had plans. Nothing more.'

'You didn't tell me that this morning! That Rick told you he likes me.'

'Did I not?'

He shrugs and spreads out his hands, the beer bottle spilling some of its contents on the snow as he does so. He quickly puts the bottle to his mouth and takes a long drink.

'If Rick ever says anything again concerning what he thinks or feels about me, would you please do me a favour and tell me?'

'Rick is my friend,' he says, defensively. 'But okay. Although I think Rick will tell you himself how he feels from now on.'

Rick is smiling at me as he walks back towards us and as stupid as it is, my heart skips a beat.

People often quote the saying that goes along the lines of, it's better to have loved and lost than to never have loved at all – or some such thing, but I have a feeling I'll be suffering for this fling for months and months to come. And that's what it is, isn't it? Or what it's going to be. Certainly as far as Rick's concerned. A fling. A hook up. Just sex.

I asked Otto if it was wise to throw us together. Maybe I should ask myself if it's wise to play this game. To pretend I'm happy to mean nothing more to Rick other than someone with whom he can briefly have a pleasant time.

The sad thing is, those people are probably right. If I have to choose between having Rick like this, or never having him at all, I think I'd choose this. I want to be with him. I want to spend time sitting in the sun with him, to eat, drink and laugh with him. And most of all, especially right now as he's walking towards me with that dynamite smile, I want to have sex with him.

'My private client is here,' Otto says to Rick.

'She's early, isn't she?'

Otto grins. 'She is keen to begin.'

Rick looks at me. 'I know how she feels.'

'Dear God,' I moan and turn away.

'Goodbye, Meg,' says Otto.

'Whatever.' I wave without turning around.

'What's wrong?' Rick asks.

'Look.' I swivel round to face him. 'I know I was the one who suggested us having sex, but let's not bring it down to school boy level, okay?'

He looks confused. 'School boy level? I'm clearly missing something. Did Otto say something that's upset you?'

'Yes! And so did you.'

'What? When? Everything was fine when I left and I've only been gone for five minutes.'

I pull a gremlin-type face and repeat what they've just said. 'Let me remind you. "She's early, isn't she?" "She is keen to begin." "I know how she feels" Ha ha ha ha. Ring any bells?'

'Not the "Ha ha ha ha" part, but the rest, yes. What's the problem?'

'You were making lewd remarks about a woman being keen to have sex, even though she might not be.'

He frowns at me. 'No I wasn't. She's keen to get on the slopes. I know how she feels. And you can believe me when I say, I know how that feels, because it's true.'

'You were looking at me when you said it. Like you're keen to ... well, you know. Have sex with me.'

He gives a snort of laughter and then coughs and scratches his head.

'Sorry. Erm. Have I walked into a parallel universe where everything's gone crazy? My remark was genuinely about her wanting to get on the slopes and ski. It's true that I want to have sex with you. I'll own up to that. I said so just now when you asked me. I've wanted to since we first met at Heathrow, if you must know. But I wasn't making a lewd remark. And the reason I was looking at you when I said that was because ... well, because I like looking at you. I'm sorry if that's a problem. I'll try not to look at you so much in future. Assuming I'll still have the chance to spend time with you. I honestly don't know why you thought what you did, but I can assure you I wasn't being lewd.'

He looks genuinely hurt that I would think that.

'Sorry. Perhaps I got the wrong end of the stick.'

He takes a long breath. 'And I'm sorry if I sounded stroppy. I think there's something I should tell you. But let's not do that here. Let's go somewhere quiet. And before you jump to any more incorrect conclusions, I'm not using this as an excuse to go somewhere for sex. I mean quiet as in, there's a load of people about to descend on this spot and I'd rather share my deepest darkest secrets away from earshot of a few dozen others.'

I turn around and Rick is right. There are several groups of skiers and snowboarders heading in our direction, and the vacant chairs around us.

'Let's go,' I say, and we hurry towards the dreaded, Zugspitze cable car, or the tin can of death as I can't help but think of it.

I'm scared before we even get on the thing, let alone start the descent, but now, after me jumping down his throat and accusing him of being lewd and childish, I'm reluctant to ask if I can hold his hand.

It's as if he can read my mind.

He leans closer and whispers, 'Please don't take this the wrong way, but would you like me to hold your hand?'

I meet his eyes, and nod. He slips his hand around mine and even with my gloves on, I can feel the comforting warmth. His hold is firm and yet gentle, and as we step into the cable car, he squeezes mine in a reassuring manner.

Queues of people behind us mean that we're moving closer to the front and as terrifying as that thought is, it's also quite exhilarating. With my hand in his I feel I can cope with anything.

'Do you want to move more towards the centre?' he asks.

'No.' I smile up at him. 'I need to face my fear.'

'I've got you,' he says, and to my surprise, he slips his free arm around my waist and pulls me closer.

Fear is a very odd thing. It can paralyze us or it can make us courageous. I know there's nothing particularly courageous about taking a cable car ride, but to those of us who aren't that comfortable with heights, doing this is like facing an army of flesh-eating aliens from another planet, and knowing we must beat them.

'Look at me, Meg,' he says, seconds before the cable car moves off.

I look into his eyes and I forget that my stomach is in my mouth, or that the soles of my feet are itching, or that my heart is racing, and my palms are sweating. His smile makes my heart swell and before I know it, I'm glancing at the view. Just for a second. And then for two. And then for three. And then I twist slightly so that I can see miles and miles of clear blue sky.

Now I look at the view ahead and every butterfly in my tummy takes flight, but they soon settle down again. Finally, I look at the valley below and I gasp. It's tiny. Either that or it's a very, very long way down.

'You've got this,' he says, as he squeezes my hand again.

And I have. I'm still nervous, and every small bump or odd noise sends a little shiver of fear through me, but by the time we reach the bottom, I'm actually just a teensy bit disappointed.

'Want to go round again?' he asks as we step out into the cold air and bright sunshine.

'Not today, thanks. But maybe one day.'

'It's a date,' he says. And oddly enough, he doesn't try to clarify that it isn't.

The path around Lake Eibsee is packed with tourists, and maybe even some locals. There are benches dotted here and there but most of those are taken.

'We could go for a walk in the forest near the chalets,' I suggest.

'I need to be sitting down to tell you this,' he says.

'Is it that bad?'

'For me to tell you, it is.'

'We could find a café somewhere, but they'll all be packed too.'

'What about Chalet Maria?' he suggests.

'Or Schloss Schatten? We'd definitely have privacy there ... if we went to your room.'

He looks me in the eye and lowers his voice so all the people around us, can't hear.

'I don't want to be accused of being lewd, or of trying to take advantage of a situation, so I'll ask you straight out to avoid confusion later. If we go to my room to talk, we'll definitely have privacy. But I want to kiss you so badly right now and if we're alone in my room, I'll want to kiss you even more. So are you saying we should go to my room for privacy and to talk? Which is fine with me. Or are you suggesting we could talk and then ... see what happens from there? You can change your mind, of course, and I'll stop the minute you ask me to, I promise. But you need to know what I'm thinking. And what I'm thinking is how much I want to hold you in my arms and explore every inch of your naked body. Am I making myself clear?'

The exhilaration I experienced on the cable car ride is nothing compared to what I'm feeling at the thought of being naked with Rick.

'Absolutely clear. And, as I think I mentioned earlier. I've got tonight off.'

He grabs my hand and the look in his eyes says it all.

'We're getting a cab to Schloss Schatten.'

Eighteen

The moment I first saw Rick at Heathrow airport I thought there was something magical in the air between us. Now I know for sure.

And it is magic on an epic scale.

The Big Bang was probably a damp squib compared to what just happened.

I think my brain may have exploded. I know my insides did. Several times.

My nerve endings are still tingling five minutes after we made love.

And yes, I know it's supposed to be sex with no emotional attachment, commitment, or promises, but it felt like love.

Like we should be together. Like we are made for one another. As corny as that might sound.

I have never experienced anything like this before; I know I probably never will again – once I go home. Rick made it abundantly clear that he does not have girlfriends, relationships, or commitments.

Only a fool would think, even for one moment, that he might change all that for me.

I may be many things, but I am not a fool.

'Are you okay?' His voice is as gentle as so many of his caresses, as he reaches out for me and pulls me closer.

His skin is damp with perspiration, as is mine, and his breathing, like my own, is still faster than it should be.

'Uh-huh,' I say.

I want to scream his name – again, as I did a few minutes ago. I've never screamed from pure pleasure before and even that was a new experience for me.

As was the way his body reacted to mine, not just in the heat of passion, but at my every touch, my every caress. It was like neither of our bodies had reached their full potential until now. Like everything and everyone else had been a square peg in a round hole, but us – we are the perfect fit.

Except of course, we're not.

I must keep reminding myself that Rick Price does not do relationships. And there are no exceptions.

'Is now a good time to talk?' he asks, turning his face towards me, and brushing a lock of hair from my eyes with his free hand, before he leans over to kiss my forehead.

We were supposed to talk before we fell into bed together, but it didn't quite work out that way. We started kissing in the cab and by the time we reached Schloss Schatten, we were desperate for one another.

Someone said hello to him as we hurried to his room, but other than a quick wave and a brief, 'Not now,' Rick didn't take much notice.

The minute we were in his room and he'd locked the door, we were tugging at each other's clothes, kissing as if we were lovers who had been apart for centuries and had just been reunited.

He did stop for a second before we were completely naked. He held my face in the palms of his hands and looked me in the eyes.

'You are sure this is what you want, aren't you? Say no now, if you've got any doubts and I'll stop.'

'Don't you dare!' I said, stretching up to kiss him. 'I want this. I want you. And yes. I know the rules. No relationships. No commitments. No promises.'

'Yes,' I say now, in answer to his question. 'It's a good time to talk. But is there any chance of some water, please?'

'Of course.' He's out of bed in a flash and brings me a bottle of water from the fridge in his room, and a glass. 'There's champagne if you prefer.'

I shake my head and he removes the bottle cap and fills the glass, which he hands to me. He gets another for himself and I gulp mine down as he gets back into bed. I can't help but admire his naked body. I've been admiring it for the last two hours, but I also noticed several scars, two of which are on his lower legs, and I assume that's where the rods are. He doesn't know that I'm aware of his accident so I'm waiting and hoping he'll tell me. If he doesn't, I can ask about the scars. It's perfectly reasonable to do so, bearing in mind how many there are and how visible each one is.

He smiles at me before he drinks his water and takes a few deep breaths before he speaks.

'You've obviously seen the scars.'

I nod but remain silent.

'I told you I'm a photographer – and I am, that's true. But I started out on a different career path when I was in my teens and it lasted until six years ago. Until I was twenty-nine.' He takes another breath, this time longer and deeper. 'Like my best friend Cody, I was a skier. Downhill was my real love but I've also competed in super G and slalom. I won the World Cup two years running and was on course to make it three, but I … I had a crash. A serious one. I broke several bones and needed some metal rods in my legs, two of which are still there today.'

'I'm so sorry, Rick. That must've been horrific. And the pain. Well, that must've been unbearable at times. Are you fully recovered now?'

He nods. 'As much as I'll ever be, physically, although I'm constantly working on building and maintaining my muscle strength. Mentally? There are still a few scars.'

'I can't begin to imagine what you've been through. What you're still going through. Does it …? I'm not sure how to ask this. Is the fact that Cody is still competing … does it make it difficult for you?'

'Am I jealous, bitter and resentful?' He smiles but it's not a smile that reaches his eyes. 'No. I hope I'm not. I was thrilled when Cody won the World Cup the year of my crash. I was thrilled about his subsequent wins, and the Gold medal. I love the fact he's done so well. And he deserves it. He's worked hard and trains hard. And he's a good man and a great friend. I want only the best for him in the future. But do I miss ski-racing? Yes. Especially during the World Championships. Do I wish the accident hadn't happened? Every single day. But life gives us challenges and we either rise to them or we crumble.'

'I'm not sure I could be as brave and as stoic as you.'

'I'm not brave. I didn't have a choice. I was ... the doctors said I might not walk again and as for skiing, forget it. But skiing was my life, or a massive part of it. I knew that one day I would have to get back on a pair of skis, however long that took. And I have. But I won't compete again. I'm told it may be possible, but if I have another crash...' He shrugs. 'I don't think it's worth the risk. So really I'm a coward.'

'No you're not!' I sit upright and stare at him in disbelief. 'How can you say that? How can you even think it?'

He smiles and this time it lights up his eyes. He gently pulls me to him and kisses me.

'Thank you for that,' he says when he releases me from his embrace.

'For what? For speaking the truth? You are much too hard on yourself, Rick Price. You charged down a mountain on a pair of skis for years and you say you're a coward? You walked again when the doctors said you wouldn't. And you've skied again. That's not a coward. That's a man of steel.'

'At least the rods in my legs are made of steel,' he jokes.

'Did you have anyone to help you heal? Family? Friends? You had Cody, of course, but anyone else?'

He glares past me into the distance, as if he's looking back in time to that period.

'I thought I had. I was wrong.' He coughs and drags his gaze to my face. 'I did have my parents and they were fantastic. They still are. They went above and beyond. And Cody was a star, in every sense. He helped me through many a dark day. I'm not sure I would've got back on skis, if not for him. He was the one who suggested I should turn my hobby of photography into a new career. He asked me to take some shots of him. I did. And I haven't stopped since then.'

'He is a true friend,' I say. 'You're lucky to have each other. Does Cody have the same philosophy on girlfriends as you?' I try to make it sound light-hearted.

'No.' He shakes his head. 'Cody has been lucky in love. And I'm pleased for him.'

'And you haven't?'

He holds my gaze. 'No. I thought I was. The truth is, I had a long-term girlfriend once. We were together for ten years. Until my accident. When the doctors said I wouldn't walk again, she decided that life with a man in a wheelchair wasn't what she'd signed up for, so she left. In a way, I understand. But also, I don't. I know I wouldn't have left her if the roles had been reversed. I decided then that I wouldn't have another serious relationship. Getting over her was almost as hard as recovering from the crash. Harder, in some ways. I don't intend to hurtle down a World Cup run again. Why would I throw myself into another relationship? I've learnt my lessons on both scores. I won't make those mistakes again.'

Now I understand. It's not really because he doesn't want a relationship. It's because he doesn't want to get his heart broken for a second time. Perhaps he is a bit of a coward, after all. But then again, the guy has been through hell, so I can't really blame him.

It's such a pity though. He's been kind and thoughtful, supportive and fun, considerate and caring, and of course, he's sensational in bed. He's the dream boyfriend. Or he would be. If his ex hadn't smashed his heart to smithereens.

One day, I hope, he'll meet someone who will help that mend and he'll open up his heart to love once more.

The annoying thing is, despite me feeling all this magic between us, that person clearly isn't me. He must've told me at least fifty times that he doesn't want a girlfriend. I might not be the brightest match in the box, but I've got the message, loud and clear.

At least one good thing will come out of it. He's asked me to have dinner here with him and his friends, tonight. That means I'll get to meet Cody Clayton, and, if I'm not mistaken, Lucinda Revere is here too.

'I'd better go back to Chalet Maria to get changed,' I say.

He grins. 'I like you just the way you are.'

'I'm naked! I don't think I should meet your friends like this, do you? And I'd like to freshen up and wear something nicer than the jeans, T-shirt and jumper I wore today.'

'They won't mind and neither do I. You looked lovely today. Which is one of the reasons why you're in my bed, naked.' The grin widens. 'Do you recall me saying that I need to constantly work on building and maintaining my muscle strength?'

'I do. But what has that got to do with me getting changed?'

'I think it's time I did a little more of the building and maintaining and you can help me with that.'

I scream with laughter as he tickles my body with little kisses before he pulls me closer and kisses me full on the mouth.

My heart is at risk of getting broken, but everything else is going far better than I ever could have dreamt.

Nineteen

I do feel a little guilty. Who wouldn't?

Rick has been open and honest with me. He's shared the story of his accident and how he felt and still feels. He's been wonderful and kind. He even insisted on walking me back to Chalet Maria so that I could change before I meet his friends and he's coming back to collect me in an hour.

What have I done in return? I've pretended that I didn't know anything about him and his friends, when in truth I did. I haven't exactly lied about what I do for a living but I haven't told the truth. I've made him believe I'm not looking for a relationship, or commitment when actually, I'd like nothing more than to be able to say he's my boyfriend. He has no idea that he's invited a wolf into his 'friendly flock' and that what I'm after is a story.

But what am I supposed to do? Either I leave here with an inside scoop, or I leave here with nothing at all. Or maybe with a broken heart.

I'll never see Rick again, and he will be fine with that. He might be disappointed or even cross that I haven't been entirely honest, but his heart won't be broken.

I'll never seen Cody or Lucinda again either. They'll get on with their wonderful lives. My story won't really hurt them. The news will come out sooner or later so what difference will it make? I won't break the story until the actual day, so their wedding won't be ruined. No real or permanent harm will be done, but something good might happen for me. I might get my dream job.

I throw off my clothes, and think of Rick, and a knot tightens around my heart. I jump in the shower and wash my hair but it doesn't make me feel better. I put on a tight-fitting navy blue dress and take extra care with my make up.

I phone Aaron for advice, without telling him I've slept with Rick, but he's no help at all.

'As I said at the start of this, I wouldn't like press intrusion on my wedding day,' he says, 'and I'm not famous. Having details of my private life splashed all over the papers and the internet isn't my idea of fun. But I understand why you're doing this and I'll try to continue to be supportive. As, I hope, I have been. Just make sure you're happy with what you're doing, Meg. Once it's out there, there's no going back.'

'I know. But how else am I going to get a decent job? I love the local paper, you know I do, but the pay isn't going to make me rich.'

'There's more to life than being rich.'

'Yeah? Tell that to Lucinda Revere, Cody Clayton, and Rick Price.'

As soon as I say it, it sounds ridiculous. Of course there's more to life than wealth. And there's more to life than having your dream career. I just haven't discovered what that is yet.

I say goodbye to my brother and I'm walking down the stairs to the hall, as Rick arrives.

'Wow!' He looks me up and down and smiles. 'You were right. It was a good idea to come and get changed. You look sensational.'

'Thank you.' I'm delighted by his comments, and once again, the guilt sets in. I shove it aside and smile. 'I'm ready when you are.'

'I'll just say hi to everyone.' He puts his head around the door of the family sitting room and Maria, Marielle, Gunter and Otto all greet him warmly.

'Enjoy your evening, Meg,' Otto says.

I peek around the door too. 'Thanks. And you.'

I've already told Marielle that I may not come back tonight but that I'll return in time to help with breakfast. She didn't ask any questions. She simply told me to have a good time, and that she wouldn't tell her mum or dad unless they asked where I was.

'They will not mind at all,' she said. 'But why tell them what they do not need to know?'

'My sentiments, exactly.'

Now, as Rick and I leave the chalet and walk hand in hand through the snow to Schloss Schatten, I don't feel so bad. All I'm doing is meeting his friends for dinner. What happens after that depends on what I think of Lucinda and Cody and how they behave tonight. If they are both arrogant, rude and self-centred, as some famous people sometimes are, especially the 'new' celebrities, I won't feel guilty any more.

'Do you have plans for New Year's Eve?' Rick asks.

'Erm. No. Other than I'll probably be working until dinner's cleared. I don't know if Maria does anything special for New Year's Eve, so I'm not sure what time I'll finish. Why?'

'Because there's a Bavarian New Year's Eve party on – you guessed it, New Year's Eve, or a guided, torchlit hike with dinner after, if that's more your style. Or, if you'd rather, we can have dinner at a restaurant and come back here and watch the fireworks.'

'That's a bit presumptuous of you, isn't it?' I tease. 'Are you saying you'd like to see me on New Year's Eve? Only if you are, I'll need to check my hectic social calendar. Seasonaires like me are in demand, you know.'

He laughs and pulls me closer to his side. 'As you've already told me you're not doing anything other than working, you've sort of shot yourself in the foot. But yes. I am saying I'd like to see you on New Year's Eve. Assuming you'd like to see me.'

'I'd like to see you naked, again,' I say.

He stops and kisses me. 'You can do that tonight if you stay with me.'

'Thanks. I'll do that.'

We walk on in silence for a few seconds and I realise there's a problem.

Rick has just said he'd like to spend New Year's Eve with me – but that's the day of this secret winter wedding. Does that mean Lucinda and Cody are getting married during the day and it'll all be over before the evening? That isn't the way famous people behave, is it? Have their wedding and then carry on as normal. Won't they be having a party? Or a dinner? Or a bash of some sort?

Unless ... maybe this is Rick's way of inviting me to the wedding as his guest, but because it's meant to be a secret, he can't tell me it's a wedding. And wasn't one of his suggestions having dinner and then returning to Schloss Schatten to watch fireworks? Perhaps there's a wedding reception at a restaurant in town and then fireworks and a party at the chalet.

'Do you have plans for tomorrow? Once you've finished your seasonaire duties for the morning.'

'No. Not really. Just more sightseeing and taking photos.'

'Then I know the perfect place to take you.' He laughs. 'Assuming your hectic social calendar is free, which once again, you've said it is. The stunning Partnach Gorge. It's open year round and if it's cold enough, the water freezes, making it pretty special and quite magical. If you've never seen cascading ice, it's impressive. It's safe, but it can get icy so you need to be careful where you walk. I'll hold your hand the entire way though.' He winks. 'Would you like to go?'

'I'd love to. Now, don't snap my head off, but by my calculations, including today, tonight, tomorrow and New Year's Eve, you'll have asked to see me four times. I realise you don't have girlfriends, or relationships, or commitments, but after four days out. Not dates. Just days out. Does that make us good friends? Friends with benefits? Or merely two people spending every day together, and, now I'm assuming, every night.'

He looks visibly uncomfortable and deep in thought.

I hastily add, 'I meant that as a joke, Rick. Don't panic.'

A smile tugs at his mouth. 'I'm not sure what that makes us. Good friends, I hope.'

'Me too. So what's for dinner? I hate to say this, but I'm starving.'

'So am I. Let's walk a little faster.'

We cover the remainder of the distance to Schloss Schatten in less than five minutes and although we laugh and talk about our favourite things to eat, there's a definite tension in the air between us. I wish I hadn't made that joke about our days out but it's too late now.

As Aaron said during our phone conversation earlier tonight. 'Once it's out there, there's no going back.'

Twenty

Lucinda and Cody couldn't be nicer if they tried. They both hug me when Rick introduces me as his friend, Meg. They tell me how lovely I look, and ask me what I'd like to drink.

Rick introduces Cody to me, as his lifelong best friend, and Lucinda as merely, Cody's girlfriend. He doesn't even call her Cody's fiancée. Lucinda doesn't seem to mind one bit, and at no time does she tell me that she is also a Mega Superstar or a pop icon. Neither does she seem annoyed or even slightly bothered that I don't appear to recognise her.

Celestine, on the other hand, couldn't be frostier when Rick introduces her as an old friend.

'Old friend? Don't you mean, former girlfriend?'

'No. I don't,' he replies, with a tight smile.

'Celestine,' Lucinda says, smiling sweetly. 'We have a guest, remember?'

Celestine curls her lip. It's deep red and plump, like a bruised plum.

'You're staying at Chalet Maria?' Lucinda asks, as Cody hands me a glass of white wine and we all sit down on the elegant and obviously expensive sofas.

'Yes,' I say. 'It's a lovely place to stay, and the family are so warm and friendly.'

'You're working as a seasonaire, I hear,' says Celestine, knocking back a glass of champagne.

'I am. And I love it. But it's only temporary.'

'That's good,' says Celestine.

I don't think she's talking about me loving the job; she's glad it's temporary.

'You're also a photographer,' Cody says, sitting as close as he possibly can to Lucinda and holding her hand in his.

'I am. It's one of the reasons I'm here.'

That much is true, at least.

'What's your surname?' asks Celestine. 'Will we have seen any of your work?'

I laugh and shake my head. 'I doubt it. Not unless you've been to Norman Landing.'

'Norman Landing?' Cody laughs. 'Is that a place, or a person?'

'A place. A seaside town on the coast of south-east England. There's an ongoing dispute over the name. It is supposed to be where William the Conqueror landed in 1066, so some think it should be, Normans' Landing with an apostrophe after the 's', and others think it should be Norman's Landing with the apostrophe between the last 'n' and the 's'. Others say it shouldn't have an 's' at all.'

'Fascinating,' Celestine says, clearly meaning the opposite.

'It gives us locals something to talk about.' I won't be fazed by her.

Rick sits next to me, but he doesn't hold my hand. Not that there is any reason why he should. We are not girlfriend and boyfriend, after all.

'I like the sound of Norman Landing,' he says. 'With or without the apostrophe or the 's'. Does it have a sandy beach?'

'No. It's pebbles. Although there is sand when the tide is out.'

'Should Cannes be worried?' Celestine raises one perfect brow.

'Probably not. But you might like it there. The amateur dramatic society is always looking for volunteers.'

If looks could kill, I would be dead.

'I'm starving,' Rick says. 'Shall we eat?'

A man dressed in a black suit and white shirt, appears from nowhere and opens a set of large double doors leading to a dining room. It makes the family dining room in Chalet Maria – and even the guest dining room, look like they belong in a doll's house. We make our way to a highly polished, curved edged, long rectangular table with two chandeliers suspended above it. I'm glad that the five of us are all seated at one end and we don't have to shout at one another along the length of it.

The man is promptly joined by two women wearing black skirts and white blouses. They're carrying trays with plates bearing our first course and it seems we're having asparagus spears wrapped in Parma ham and drizzled with hollandaise sauce. Not quite what I was expecting, but one of my favourite starters. Service is formal and exemplary and each of the four courses is delicious.

Dinner conversation is polite and friendly with the odd barb thrown at me by Celestine. But at no time does anyone allude to Lucinda's iconic status or even Cody's fame and as ludicrous as it may be, I don't mention it either. It's as if we all know that they are who they are so there's no need to discuss it. I only discover Celestine is a famous catwalk model when I see her photo in an open magazine on the coffee table after dinner, but the next time I look, the magazine is closed.

We discuss Christmas, the weather, GaPa and its many attractions, including everything connected with The Alpine Ski World Cup and the Four Hills tournament, but still not the fact that Cody's a World Cup holder, although he does admit that he fractured his wrist whilst skiing recently.

Which takes us on to how Rick and Cody have been lifelong friends and how they met when Cody's parents moved to Aspen, Colorado when Cody was three years old. So not quite *lifelong* friends then, but pretty close.

That's how I learn that Aspen is where Rick grew up and where his parents still live. And that the reason he was at Heathrow airport when we first met was because this year, his folks have been spending Christmas with other relatives in a place called Virginia Water, an affluent village in Surrey in England, and that Rick had gone to join them for a few days.

I ask where Cody was born and am surprised by his reply.

I wouldn't think a downhill skier would be thrilled to be named after a town called Cody Falls. Falling is dangerous at the speeds downhill skiers race down a mountain, as both Rick and Cody know only too well. If it were me, I'd see *Cody Falls* as a bad omen, but of course, when his parents named him, they didn't know what career he would grow up to pursue. If they had, I'm sure they would've chosen differently, but Cody seems proud of his namesake, and either the irony of it escapes him or it simply doesn't bother him at all.

'I was named after the town, but Mom tells everybody that the town was named after me. Cody Falls was there long before I was born. It was named after the Codene family,' he continues. 'They settled there in 1859 after gold was discovered nearby during the Colorado Gold Rush. They used the waterfall as a shower and the cave behind was where they lived until the Codene men built their cabin.' A smile sweeps across his face and he leans closer to me and gives my elbow a tiny nudge. 'Don't tell Mom I said that.'

'My lips are sealed,' I say, glad that this is one secret I can easily keep. Although, it might add an extra point of interest to my story.

Celestine was born in London, England – but no one cares about her. At least I don't.

Lucinda, I've read, was born in Bristol, which is also in England, but she now says she was born in Bath, although that's only about twelve miles or so away from Bristol. Unless I misheard her and she said she was born *in a bath*. I somehow doubt that. But that would definitely add interest to my story.

Before I met her, I expected Lucinda to be knocking back champagne or vodka shots or some such thing, but all she drinks all evening is water with dinner, and herbal tea before she goes to bed. And she goes to bed early, at 10 p.m. which astonishes me. She's only twenty-five. She should be up till all hours.

'I hope you won't mind if I leave you to it,' she says. 'I've been feeling tired lately and my doctor tells me I need some early nights. It was lovely to meet you and I look forward to seeing you again very soon.'

'I don't mind at all,' I say. 'Feel better. It was lovely to meet you too. And I also hope to see you again before I return to the UK.'

'When do you leave?' she asks.

'On January 4th.'

She looks surprised. 'Oh! That really is soon, but we'll definitely meet again before then. I don't suppose I'll see you in the morning because I tend to sleep in till at least 8 a.m. and Rick says you've got an early start.'

'She's staying the night?' Celestine sounds horrified. 'Am I the last to know everything around here?'

Everyone ignores her.

I'm astonished Rick told them I was staying, but maybe he has to tell the owners if anyone stays over who isn't, strictly speaking, a guest at Schloss Schatten.

I'm also intrigued by the fact that there don't seem to be any other guests staying here. But I suppose with Lucinda's money she can afford to rent the entire place for as long as she likes. It must be lovely to have that much cash.

Soon after Lucinda goes to bed, Cody says goodnight. He adds that he too looks forward to seeing me again but he also tells me not to take any nonsense from his best friend.

'He's got a heart of gold,' Cody says, slapping Rick on the arm with his uninjured hand.

'Go to bed,' says Rick, 'or I'll break your other wrist, but they're both grinning like Cheshire cats.

'I'm going out,' says Celestine. 'Don't wait up.'

As if we would. But I am taken aback when she adds that she's meeting Otto, especially as she doesn't sound that thrilled at the prospect. And I'm astounded by what Rick tells me, once she's left – that Otto is her ex.

'They dated five years ago, which is when Cody and I met her. She was one of Otto's private clients and we've known Otto for years. They've had an on and off relationship ever since. But last year, Otto told her it was over for good and that's when she and I ... hooked up, once or twice. I soon realised Otto wasn't as over her as he made out, so I stopped seeing her immediately, but she seems to have formed a bit of a thing for me and she just won't shake it off. It's awkward because she's a good friend of Lucinda's, even though they're as different as chalk and cheese. That's how Lucinda and Cody met. Celestine brought Lucinda here, to this very chalet, four years ago this Christmas, during one of Celestine and Otto's 'off' periods. Celestine introduced Lucinda to us and it was obvious right away that Cody and Lucinda liked one another. By the end of her holiday, they had fallen in love.'

Now I understand why they're having their wedding in GaPa. This is the place they met and fell in love. I'm even more convinced that the wedding reception is at this chalet. And that as unbelievable as it seems, I may have got an invitation – albeit a secret one.

'And talking of liking one another,' Rick continues, as that dynamite smile spreads across his lips and he shifts closer to me on the sofa. 'I could do with an early night. How about you?'

I smile at him as sexily as possible. 'I think I'll stay up for a bit.' I laugh at his obvious disappointment. 'If you believe that you'll believe anything. I've been longing to be back in your bed for at least the last two hours. Not that your friends aren't lovely and great company. They are. But they're not as great as you. And besides, now that I'm aware of your need to work on your muscle strength, I feel I have a responsibility to help with that in any way I can.'

'Do you?' His smile is mesmerising. 'I can think of several ways you can help. And they all involve getting naked as soon as humanly possible.'

Twenty-one

'How long have the Messy Girls been staying here?' I ask Marielle as we're cleaning the guest's rooms this morning.

I didn't get much sleep last night and although I had a fantastic time, I'm slightly frazzled now when greeted by the chaos in their room. Not only does it look as if they're holding a jumble sale, it looks as if they've been burgled and there's been a chemical explosion in their ensuite.

'This will be their third week,' Marielle says, shaking her head and sighing. 'You will need help with this.'

'No. Please don't worry. I'll be fine.'

I pick up all the clothes, bags and shoes strewn across the floor, together with two devices; a mobile phone, and a laptop that is open and, it seems, on which the screen is frozen on what appears to be a photo-editing software program. I only notice that, because

I recognise the logo of the program, and also, the man in the photo that is frozen.

It's a photo of Cody Clayton ... in what I can only describe as a compromising position.

It's a recent photo because, on the arm that's in the air in an unsuccessful attempt to stop the picture from being taken, there's a bandage on his wrist. Not only did Cody fracture his wrist in his skiing accident, he gashed it open, hence the bandage. In reports I read it said he had five stitches on the wound.

He's smiling in the photo, so whoever took it must know him – and know him well enough for him not to be annoyed, even though he doesn't like his photo being taken. But more importantly, for him to be naked at the time, save for a portion of sheet which is covering his nether regions, on the bed he's lying on.

And even more important than all of that is the fact that he's lying on that bed with a stunningly beautiful but heavily made-up young woman – and it definitely is *not* Lucinda Revere.

Yet, apart from the obvious and despicable fact that he's been cheating on Lucinda, there's something about the photo that doesn't seem quite right.

Don't ask me why – because I know it's personal property and I shouldn't have – I pull my phone from my pocket and take a photo of the screen. I close the laptop and place it on the coffee table with the other one. I think that's where they fell from but I don't know how they fell. Was there a fight or something in this room? That would explain the mess.

Should I tell Marielle about the laptop? Or Rick? Or Cody? Or Lucinda? Doesn't she deserve to know that Cody's not the man he appears to be? He's not the attentive, loyal and loving partner she thinks he is. He's a liar and a cheat.

Look who's talking? But I wouldn't cheat on my partner.

Unless Lucinda knows what Cody's like and can live with it. Some women seem able to forgive a cheating lover. I am not one of those women and never will be. I draw a line at some things.

It's really none of my business so perhaps I should forget I saw it.

I can't stop thinking about it though, and all morning I have a feeling of unease, as if I'm aware of something that's about to happen but I don't know what it is.

When Rick arrives to collect me, I consider showing him the photo on my phone, but he's a little distracted so maybe it's best to wait.

Partnach Gorge is as stunning as Rick told me yesterday it would be. The gorge is deep and narrow and the trail passes along ledges above the river, and weaves through odd shaped galleries and tunnels. In places, the water is frozen and the cascading ice is definitely a sight worth seeing. I take a lot of photos as does Rick. Today he's brought his camera and together with photos of the gorge, he takes a lot of photos of me, so I take some of him. At least I'll have those to remember him.

'I was going to take you to the summit of Mount Wank,' he says when we leave the gorge.

'Mount Wank? Are you serious?'

He laughs and nods his head. 'Yes. It's the one opposite Zugspitze and has a panoramic view of GaPa and the mountains, but the cable car is closed for maintenance, so we'll go somewhere else for coffee and cake instead.'

'Could we go back to Zugspitze and take the cable car both up and back down?'

'Wow. You really are facing your fears and smashing them aren't you?'

'Yes. Plus, it's another glorious day and I'd like to sit in the sunshine. When I go back home, I'll miss the mountain views so I'd like to breathe in as much mountain air as I can.'

'Your wish is my command.'

'Is everything all right?' I ask as we make our way towards the cable car. 'You seem a little … tense today. Are you getting bored with me already because if so you–'

'Bored with you? Are you mad? Sorry. But the last thing I am is bored with you. I am a bit cross today but it has nothing to do with you.' He sighs and runs a hand through his hair. 'That's not strictly true.' He stops and places his hand on my arm to turn me to face him. 'I'm not sure I should be telling you this but knowing Celestine, she'll tell you if she gets a chance and I'd rather you hear it from me.'

'Is this about Cody?'

Has his cheating been exposed?

'Cody?' Rick's brows knit together. 'No. Why would you think that?'

'No reason.'

'It's about Celestine. And you. And me, I suppose.'

I didn't expect that.

'O-kay. What is it?'

He lets out a breath. 'Celestine's lost her phone. She had it last night at dinner but this morning she couldn't find it. It's ridiculous, of course, and we've proved she's wrong, but … well … she said she thought you took it.

Don't get upset. We all told her she was being an idiot and unkind and that she must've lost it last night when she was out, but she wouldn't let it drop. I phoned Otto to ask if she had it when she met him and luckily, he said she had, but she still insists you could've taken it this morning and we can't prove she didn't have it when she came home. I assured her you were with me the entire time, both last night and this morning and that as we even showered together, you weren't alone for a moment, but that made her angry. I walked you back to Chalet Maria, so you didn't even leave on your own.'

I'm speechless for a moment but finally I manage, 'I didn't take her bloody phone! Why would I? You do believe me, don't you?'

'Yes! Of course I do. We all do – apart from Celestine. I think ... I think she's annoyed with me and she's taking it out on you. I'm so sorry Meg.'

'Is she ... does she really believe I took it?'

Dear God! The bloody woman might call the police and then what will happen? They'll check up on me and discover I've been lying about what I do for a living, and then they might think I'm lying about this. How can this be happening?

He shrugs. 'I don't know. But we know you didn't. Celestine says we don't know anything about you and you could be a thief who targets people like us.' He laughs. 'What can I say? She can be a little crazy. And overly dramatic.'

'If I were, I would've taken more than her bloody phone! How dare she accuse me of this. I've never been so insulted in my life.'

He takes my hands in his and pulls me into a hug, before looking me in the eyes.

'Please don't be upset. I knew I shouldn't have said anything. We know you didn't do it. It'll turn up, you wait and see. And we'll insist Celestine apologises to you, believe me.'

'And when the police knock on my door? What then?'

'They won't.'

'They will if she accuses me of this.'

He shakes his head. 'We told her to simply report it as missing, and not to mention you. Hundreds of phones go missing every day, so the police won't do anything about it. What can they do? Honestly, just forget it. I only told you because, if we go back to the chalet later, Celestine might confront you, even though she's been warned not to.'

'Warned not to?'

'Yes. By me, and by Cody and Lucinda.'

'Great! And I was having such a lovely day.'

'I've ruined it haven't I?'

'Celestine has ruined it?'

And she could ruin everything. What if she looks me up on the internet? She doesn't know my surname because I didn't tell her when she asked last night, but all she has to do is search for Meg and Norman Landing. All my articles and photos and my advice column, will pop up on her screen. She can then blow my cover and I can say goodbye to my story – and to Rick, when he finds out I've been lying.

And, they might all believe it *was* me who stole her damn phone.

Why didn't the woman take better care of it?

The ride in the cable car wasn't quite as thrilling after that. Nor was sitting in the sunshine, or eating lunch in the restaurant. I didn't even feel like having sex, but part of me wanted to show Celestine that I wouldn't be intimated by her.

When Rick asked me in the cable car on the way back down what I wanted to do next and if there was something he could do to cheer me up, I said, 'Yes. You can take me home to Schloss Schatten.'

'Are you sure?' he queried.

'Absolutely.'

'I'm glad. Not only because I want to spend more time with you but also because it proves you're a strong woman who won't take crap from anyone. And I like that.'

'Will you like it when I punch Celestine on her nose?' He looked a bit concerned, until I added, 'Don't worry. I'm not a physically violent person. As tempting as it might be to do it.'

'I'm not sure I'd blame you if you did,' he said, with a half smile. 'I was pretty tempted to do so myself this morning. But don't you worry either. Because I wouldn't do that anymore than you would.'

I can't tell you how relieved I am when, on arrival at Schloss Schatten, Lucinda beams at Rick and me, and gives us the good news.

'Celestine's phone has been handed in!'

She is almost as happy as me, but I try to remain calm.

'That's good.'

Rick's happy too. 'Good? It's fantastic news. I know I said that it would turn up, but I thought it had probably gone forever. People don't often hand in things like mobile phones. Especially not expensive ones, like hers.' He squeezes my hand. 'Now she can apologise.'

Lucinda blinks twice. 'You told Meg?'

He throws her a contrite smile. 'I was worried that Celestine would confront her if we came back here. And in a way, Meg has a right to know if someone accuses her of such an awful thing.'

'But none of us believed it.' Lucinda casts me a pleading look. 'We didn't, Meg. We knew it wasn't you. We were sure she lost it somewhere last night.'

'Thanks,' I say. 'It's good to know that people trust me. At least, some people do.'

The twinge of guilt flares in my stomach and I feel a little queasy. Who am I to be talking about trust? I'm lying through my teeth. I thought this would be so much easier than it is.

But Cody is a liar too. I mustn't forget that.

'I need a whisky,' Rick says, heading for the cocktail bar in the corner of the sitting room. 'Would you like one, Meg?'

'Not a whisky, thanks. But a glass of wine or something would be great.'

'Water for you?' He smiles at Lucinda as he pours my wine and his whisky.

'Yes please. I thought today was going to be awful, but I'm so happy that it won't be.'

'Where's Cody this afternoon?' I ask, thinking about the photo I had seen.

'He's taken Celestine to retrieve her phone. They should be back any moment.'

As if on cue, a moment later, Celestine and Cody walk in. Celestine stops dead and stares at me. She has the decency to blush and look a little ashamed.

Cody doesn't seem surprised to see me, and smiles, before hurrying to Lucinda's side and sitting next to her on the sofa. He takes her hand in his and kisses it.

The queasy feeling in my stomach returns. Now that I know he's a cheat, I don't feel the same way about him, and I'm not sure I can pretend I do.

'I hear your phone was handed in,' Rick says, glaring at Celestine.

'It was.' She coughs. 'It was handed in at lunchtime.'

'Where?' He continues to glower at her.

'It was given to the manager of one of the clubs Otto and I went to last night.'

'So you did lose it last night and not this morning.'

'Yes.'

'You owe Meg an apology.'

Her eyes open wide and her perfect brows shoot upwards.

'You told her?'

'I thought it was better coming from me. I wish I hadn't now, because it ruined our day. Maybe next time, Celestine, you'll think long and hard before you accuse someone of doing something, without any evidence to support it.'

'Fine.' She glares at me. 'I'm sorry. Okay?'

I could cause a scene, but those in glass houses shouldn't throw stones, so instead I smile and nod my head in acceptance.

'Apology accepted,' I say. 'I'm glad you got it back. We keep so much on our phones, that losing them is like losing part of us.'

'Yes!' she says, she actually smiles at me. 'I would die without my phone. That's why I was so upset this morning. I shouldn't have accused you. I am sorry.'

'No permanent harm done.' I return her smile, but I'll continue to be wary of her.

She puts her phone on the coffee table as Rick passes Cody a beer.

'May I have a glass of wine please?' she purrs, as she heads towards the door.

'I'm tempted to tell you to get it yourself,' Rick says, but he's smiling. 'Are you seriously going to leave your phone on the coffee table? You'll be losing it again and next time you'll probably accuse the staff.'

'I won't! And I'm only going to the loo. I'll be back in five minutes.'

'Honestly.' Rick tuts, as he goes back to the cocktail bar and pours her a glass of wine.

'At least we all know what her phone looks like,' says Lucinda.

'It looks like any other phone,' Rick says.

'No it doesn't.' Lucinda laughs. 'Okay. We obviously *don't* all know what her phone looks like. Look at the case on the back.'

Rick flips the phone over when he puts Celestine's glass of wine on the table beside it.

'Oh yes. I've never noticed that before, and I must've seen this phone a hundred times.'

'What?' Cody asks, leaning forward.

Rick holds it up for Cody to see, and then, when Cody nods and pulls a knowing face, Rick shows the phone to me.

It takes me a second until I spot the tiny, sparkling stones across the bottom of the cover, spell out a name. But it isn't Celestine's.

'Who is Beatrice?' I ask.

'It's her gran,' Lucinda says. 'Or at least, it was. She passed away the same year my own mum died. I had this ring made out of my mum's ashes.'

She holds out her hand for me to see the diamond ring she's wearing on the third finger of her right hand. Cody and Rick have obviously seen it before. And now I notice that the third finger of her left hand is bare. I didn't spot that last night. I thought she was supposed to be Cody's fiancée. What is going on?

'I'm so sorry for your loss,' I say. 'The ring is beautiful.'

'Thank you. Mum died several years ago. The year before I met Cody.' She smiles at him and he smiles back with genuine love in his smile. 'That's why Celeste brought me here that year. It was the first Christmas without my mum. My Dad died years ago, a few weeks before I was born so I would've been alone if not for Celestine.'

'That would've been very hard.'

'Yes. Instead, I met Cody and fell in love.' She beams at him again and this time he kisses her cheek. 'Celestine had her gran's ashes made into those tiny diamonds and fixed to that cover, which fits all the phones she buys. I told her she might lose it, but she says it's okay, because she has more of Beatrice's ashes at home, and Beatrice loved to travel.' She shakes her head and laughs.

Wow. I understand why Celestine was so upset. It wasn't just her phone she was losing; it was also part of her gran.

And now I also know that, not only does Celestine have a heart, and that she takes care of her friends, she also has a sense of humour. I'm not sure which surprises me the most.

Twenty-two

I tell Marielle of the saga with Celestine's phone as we're about to start serving afternoon tea for the guests.

'She accused you of stealing?' Marielle is horrified. 'I cannot believe how much Celestine has changed since we first met her. She was so nice when Otto started dating her.' She raises her eyes to meet mine. 'You are aware they dated?'

'Yes. Rick told me.'

'Ah yes. Rick. He also … spent time with Celestine.' She shakes her head. 'I like Rick very much. My entire family likes him. But he is strange since his accident. Oh. You know of his accident?'

'Yes. He told me all about it.'

'Rick says he does not date. But he does. He just will not call it dating. It is as if the word dating is a knife in his heart.'

'I think that's probably because his ex-girlfriend broke his heart, and now he'll do anything to stop it getting broken again.'

'But by doing this, he breaks other people's hearts. And yet he cannot see this.'

I nod. 'I know. But are you saying Rick broke Celestine's heart? Or that Otto did?'

Marielle shrugs. 'I think Otto broke it, and then Rick crumpled the pieces. Love is difficult. Celestine is ... high maintenance, as people call it when a person needs constant attention. Otto grew tired of this. But he loved her and so they dated and parted, over and over, until Otto made their parting final. Celestine turned to Rick, and he picked up the pieces, but made it clear they had no future. Celestine craves love. Perhaps we all do. But she chases love away. Otto still loves her. I am sure of it. Rick saw this. Otto does not. Celestine loves Otto, but believes she loves Rick. As I said, love is difficult.'

'Tell me about it! That's an expression, not a request.' I laugh. 'It sounds complicated. But Celestine and Otto went out together last night, didn't they?'

'Yes. But they are not dating. I am told by Otto that Celestine was cross because he was talking to two women Celestine did not know. He explained they are guests of our chalet and yet she was still cross, and drank so much that Otto had to take her home to Schloss Schatten.'

'Oh dear. And she lost her phone. At least she has that back now. What about you, Marielle? Is there anyone you're interested in?'

'No. I thought once, that Cody and I...' Her voice trails off.

'You dated Cody?'

She nods. 'For a time. It did not last. And now he loves Lucinda.'

'Do you still care for him?'

'Yes. But as a friend. Nothing more. I wish them much happiness.'

'I think the guests are back,' I say. I can hear voices and laughter and doors slamming and banging. 'Shall I make the drinks?'

'Yes please. I will take the cakes.'

I make two pots of tea, pour coffee into two serving pots from the main jug, and make two pots of hot chocolate. I carry them into the guest sitting room which is where afternoon tea is served.

Raucous laughter batters my eardrums. The messy girls are enjoying themselves it seems. I place the drinks on the sideboard where Marielle has put the cakes, beside the cups and saucers and plates, for the guests to help themselves. As I turn to walk back towards the kitchen the messy girls head for the hot chocolate.

'The photo's really good,' one of them says. 'Do you think it'll do the job?'

'Shush!' says the other one. 'Someone might hear.'

'Who?' says the first, as if I'm invisible.

It's funny how some people do that. Behave as if people who serve others are not really there.

But I am there and I do hear them. And it reminds me of the photo I saw on one of their laptops this morning when I picked it up from the floor, along with one of their phones. Which now I come to think of it again, was similar to Celestine's.

I stop in my tracks and spin around to look at them.

It wasn't similar to Celestine's phone. Unless I am very much mistaken, it *was* Celestine's phone! I remember the little diamonds on the back, which I thought were stick-on crystals at the time and I didn't pay them any attention. I didn't notice they spelt out a name.

'What?' says one of them, realising I'm looking at them.

'Nothing,' I say. 'I was just wondering what it is you want.'

'Some privacy,' she says with a smirk. 'And get us two glasses of wine while you're at it.'

'I'm sorry. Alcohol is only served at dinner.'

I hurry to the kitchen. What should I do? Why did these women have Celestine's phone? Assuming it was her phone and not an almost identical one.

Didn't Marielle just say two women from this chalet were making Celestine jealous? And that Otto took her home. Perhaps it was the messy girls and they took her phone when he and Celestine weren't looking. But why?

And what was the business about a photo? That sounded a bit dodgy.

Hold on. Were they talking about the photo of Cody I saw this morning on the laptop in their room? Was that laptop stolen too? And maybe, like Celestine's phone, returned later. But from whom? And again, why?

None of this makes any sense.

I try to picture the photo but I can't.

Wait. I took a photo of it.

I tell Marielle I need the loo and I quickly take a peek at my phone. The photo is there and I stare at it, making sections of it bigger by scrolling out with my thumb and forefinger. The girl's face is half hidden by

Cody's hand and arm but it definitely isn't Lucinda. I know the face though.

God! I am so stupid. Of course I know the face. It's just smirked at me and asked me for wine. It's one of the messy girls.

Oh yuk! Why did Cody have to sleep with one of them? I don't think they're nice people.

A call distracts me from my thoughts. It's my brother Aaron.

'Hi Aaron. Everything okay? I can't talk long. I should be working.'

'Everything's fine. I'm just checking how things are going with you and this secret winter wedding stuff. Oh, and I want to run something by you. But tell me about the wedding first.'

'Not a lot to report, sadly. But lots of other stuff is happening and it's all very confusing.'

'Erm. Isn't the wedding supposed to be on New Year's Eve?'

'Yes. So Tori said. But Lucinda's not wearing a ring. There's no sign of any guests, or anything at all to suggests a wedding of any sort is going to take place here.'

'It's New Year's Eve tomorrow. You're running out of time.'

'I'm well aware of that, but thank you for stating the obvious.'

'I have to say, Meg, I think there's more chance of an extinction level comet hitting the Earth than there is of you getting a scoop about this so called secret winter wedding.'

'Thank you for your support. But it means there is still a chance. After all, an extinction level comet wiped out the dinosaurs, I believe, but you clearly survived.'

'Funny. Well, good luck with it. Seriously. I mean that.'

'Thanks Aaron. I know you do. So what's this thing you want to run by me?'

He clears his throat. 'Emma is coming back just after New Year's Day.'

'Katie's sister Emma, you mean? Yes I know she is.'

'Her place only has two bedrooms.'

'I know.' I sigh. 'Aaron? Why are you telling me things I already know?'

'Just listen, will you?'

'Fine.'

'Nan is also staying at Emma's, and Nan's boyfriend Donald's also there most of the time now.'

'Oh, I see. It's getting a bit cramped. And when Emma comes back it'll be more cramped. Are you asking if Katie can come and stay with me? Because she can.'

'No. I'm ... I want to ask Katie to come and stay with me. Only I'm worried she might think it's too soon. I love her so much and I don't want to blow this.'

I burst out laughing. 'Oh, Aaron! I do love you! Katie adores you. Anyone can see that. And yes, I know you've only been dating for a matter of days but love is love and you're both head over heels. I say go for it. If you're worried she'll panic – which I don't think she will, you could offer her the guest room and tell her she can take things slowly if she wants. But you slept together on Christmas Eve and no doubt every night since, so I don't think there'll be a problem. I honestly think she'll jump at the chance to move in with you. Congratulations!'

'Do you really think so?'

'Yes. Just don't propose to her yet. Actually, forget I said that. If you want to propose to her, do it.'

'I do want to propose to her. But I'll wait. I can't really believe this is happening, It hasn't sunk in yet. I keep expecting to wake up and discover it's all been a dream. I know I want to spend my life with her but I don't want to rush things. I'll give her a week or two to settle in.' He laughs.

'I'm so happy for you both. But I must get on, so I'll call you tomorrow. Give my love to Katie, and to Mum and Dad. And give Ember a hug from me.' I blow kisses down the phone and jump up and down with happiness once he's rung off.

I'm thrilled my brother has finally found love again after being broken hearted for so long.

There's hope for everyone. I just know it.

But he's right about this damn wedding. They are keeping this thing so secret that no one seems to know about it. Tori's boss is supposed to be a guest, yet I haven't seen or heard anything about him. Tori showed me his photo so I'll recognise him if he arrives. I should've asked where he was staying. She said she had made all his travel arrangements. I'll give her a call later.

I finish afternoon tea service and help Marielle clear the things away, after which, she and Maria wander off into the pantry to check supplies and I decide to take a five-minute break in the family sitting room. It'll soon be time to prepare dinner but for now I can relax.

I'm drinking a cup of hot chocolate, seated in one of the armchairs in front of the large windows and admiring the views, when my phone rings once again. This time it's Rick.

'Hello,' I say, pleased to hear his voice, after only being away from him for a few hours.

'Hello, you.' He sounds just as happy. 'Are you busy?'

'Dreadfully. I'm rushed off my feet. Maria is a slave driver.' I chuckle. 'Actually, I'm drinking delicious hot chocolate, sitting in a comfy chair and looking out the window. What about you?'

'I'm doing something similar. And calling you. I know you should be working this evening, but there's a little celebration at this chalet tonight and I'd like you to come as my guest. Only a few people. Nothing fancy. Oh ... can you line dance?'

'Can I what? Line dance? No. But I can watch.'

'No chance. You'll be fine. I'll show you the ropes.'

'There are ropes?'

He roars with laughter. 'No. But there could be later if you play your cards right.'

'Promises, promises.'

'God, Meg! How do you do that?'

'Do what?'

'Make me want to make love to you every five minutes.'

'It's a gift.'

'You're telling me it is. You're the best gift I've had in a long time. Can you get off early and we'll sneak in a muscle building work out too?'

'I'll see what I can do. Do you want me to spend the night?'

'Do you really need to ask?'

'Yes. It's only polite.'

'Then the answer is a very polite, yes, please. What time shall I come and get you?'

'Can I text you later? I'll have to ask Maria and Marielle.'

'They're invited too.'

'To the celebration?'

'Yep. Cody's calling them now.'

'Really? What is this little celebration for?'

'It's a secret. I'll explain when you get here.'

'Not when you come to collect me?'

'No. You'll have to be patient.'

'I'm not very good at that.'

'It's great to know you're not good at everything.'

'I'm not very good at many things.'

'You're kidding? You're good with people. You're brilliant at making me happy. You're sensational in bed. You're a fantastic photographer. You're great at everything that matters as far as I can tell.'

'You're the one who's great at everything. But I'm delighted you think so highly of me. I hope ... I hope I won't disappoint you tonight.'

'I don't think you could ever disappoint me, Meg. Is something wrong?'

'No. Everything is … going perfectly. I can't wait to find out what this secret is all about.'

'I can't wait to tell you. Text me later. I'm already looking forward to seeing you.'

I love Rick's voice. I could listen to it all day.

But is it just his voice I love? I shift in my chair. I mustn't think like that.

'Same here,' I say, and I ring off with a huge smile on my face.

Finally! Something to confirm there is a secret wedding. Or at least a secret something.

Rick's invitation to this 'little celebration' suggests it is a wedding. I must remember to take my camera. Now he's said I'll be spending the night, I can say it's just my overnight bag, and maybe I can sneakily take some photos, while no one is looking. Although I do need them to be looking in my general direction so that I can get face-shots. Or at the very least, profiles.

But wait.

The secret winter wedding is supposed to be tomorrow, not tonight.

Unless this was the plan all along. Perhaps they knew word would get out and they decided to have the wedding the day before anyone expects them to.

Either way, it'll be me who gets the inside scoop, thanks to Rick.

I finish my hot chocolate and ponder.

He's probably going to hate me afterwards.

But we don't have a future together anyway, so is that a problem?

I push myself out of the chair and walk towards the kitchen.

Why do I feel it is?

Why do I feel like an awful person?

A cheat and a liar.

But I'm not the cheat and liar. Cody is.

I shove the kitchen door open but no one's there yet. I put my cup in the dishwasher and lean against the worktop.

Lucinda might be marrying Cody tonight. Unless I do something to make her aware of what he's like.

But should I do that?

Do I have the right to do that?

Is it any of my business?

Whether they have a wedding or a massive row, it'll be a front-page story, so I'll get a scoop no matter what.

I wash my hands and dry them.

Why then, do I just want Lucinda and Cody to have a happy ever after?

Is it because that's what we all want?

My brother Aaron is getting his happy ever after with Katie and I'm over the moon about it.

Am I feeling conflicted about Lucinda and Cody because I believe they deserve one too, in spite of Cody cheating?

Is it because I want a happy ever after of my own?

Fat chance of that happening.

Rick Price doesn't believe in happy ever afters.

He doesn't even believe in dating.

Despite all the wonderful things he says.

Twenty-three

'I've never line-danced before, but Rick assures me it isn't that difficult.'

Marielle raises her brows. 'Does he?'

Why do I have the feeling Rick may not be telling me the entire truth about that?

We're waiting for the rest of Marielle's family to come and join us in their sitting room, before we head off to this 'little celebration'. Unbeknownst to me, and it seems to everyone in Marielle's family apart from Otto, catering staff from outside have been booked to come in and serve the guests tonight. Bruno, the chef, will cook dinner as usual, but the hired staff will do service, clear up and do everything else that normally needs to be done, giving Marielle, Maria, Gunter and Otto, oh, and me, the evening off. Which means, Otto must've known about this celebration a while ago, because it's New Year's Eve tomorrow and even tonight, catering staff would be hard to find at short notice.

'Is it, hard?' I ask Marielle, still concerned I'm going to make a complete and utter fool of myself at this line-dancing shindig.

She smiles sympathetically. 'I think you will soon find out. Some people take to it like a dog to water.'

'Erm. I think you mean like a duck to water. But in my case, you're probably right about the dog. Can you line-dance?'

'Oh yes. We have had many American guests over the years, and it is popular. And, of course, we are friends with Rick and Cody.'

'So I'll be the only beginner then? Oh joy.'

'Perhaps not. There may be others at the party who do not know how.'

'Do you know what this little celebration is for?'

Marielle glances at Maria who's just joined us in the sitting room.

'No. Otto may, I believe, but he will not say. Like you, Mama, Papa and I are … in the dark.'

'It is snowing,' says Maria. 'Heavily.'

She points to the windows and although it's almost 7 p.m. and it's dark outside, the lights from the chalet and nearby, show us she's right. It's coming down like the icing sugar I sifted over the sponge cake this afternoon ... only more so.

'That doesn't bode well for other guests going to this party,' I say. 'How will they all get there?'

For us, it's only a few minutes walk through the forest to reach Schloss Schatten, although in these conditions even that will be a bit of a trudge. Others may be coming from far and wide. I know transport in and around GaPa is good and used to coping with weather like this, but Chalet Maria and Schloss Schatten are halfway up a mountain, or at least, several hundreds of metres above the town.

'Do not worry,' says Marielle. 'I'm sure Rick and Cody will have thought of that. It does snow here a lot in winter.'

'Of course. Should I tell Rick not to come and meet me and that I'll make my way to Schloss Schatten with you and your family?'

'I will ask Otto what is planned,' Maria says, and promptly calls out his name.

A few moments later, he saunters into the room, looking like he's just stepped off a movie set for a stylish Western. He's wearing smart jeans, a fabulously fringed checked shirt, a large leather belt, leather cowboy boots and a ten-gallon hat.

'Wow!' I say. 'Don't you look a picture?'

'Is that a compliment?' he queries.

'Yes, sir, it is.' I may soon discover I'm rubbish at line-dancing but no one can say I'm not getting into the spirit of the wild west.

'And the accent is supposed to be American?' He looks sceptical.

'Everyone's a critic, boy,' I say in an old prospector's voice. Or how I imagine an old prospector would have talked.

Marielle, Maria and Otto look perplexed, but Gunter, who joins us in time to hear it, laughs. He's also dressed as a cowboy, but he's not as smooth-looking as Otto. Marielle and Maria are wearing pretty, floral dresses; Maria's is below the knee, Marielle's is short, showing off her long legs. They're both also wearing cowboy boots and I'm aware that I'm the odd one out. I am wearing a dress, but it's a plain, dark red, midi-length shirt dress, the buttons open from just above my knee. I don't have cowboy boots. I hadn't realised they'd be needed in a ski resort in Germany. I'm wearing my fur-lined, snow boots, but I've got shoes in my overnight bag that I'll change into at Schloss Schatten.

'Should we wait for Rick,' Maria asks Otto, 'or leave now?'

'Rick will be here in a few minutes with a skimobile to take Meg. Papa will take you on his and I will take Marielle on mine.'

'You have skimobiles?' I haven't seen them so I'm surprised.

Otto gives me a look that tells me I should've known they had. 'Of course. We have a lot of snow here in winter.'

'Yes. So I've been told.'

Otto's phone beeps and he glances at the screen. 'Ah. Rick is here. We shall go now.'

I've never ridden a snowmobile before tonight so it's another new experience for me. I'm already in two minds as to whether or not it's one I'd like to repeat, because it's both exhilarating and terrifying. The journey through the forest from Chalet Maria to Schloss Schatten will only take a couple of minutes at the speed we're travelling, but with three snowmobiles racing across the snow and weaving between the trees, it's going to be a few hair-raising minutes. At least it is for me. Or it would be – if I didn't have a helmet shoved on my recently perfectly coiffed hair. The ski goggles don't improve my make-up, but I suppose they do stop my mascara from streaking, and me from being blinded by the heavily falling snow, as we bounce along. Although, as I'm clinging to Rick for dear life, I'll probably have an imprint of his jacket on my face, from where my cheek is pressed against his back. The trip is also quite noisy. And bumpy. But in a way it's fun.

I panic slightly when we start racing downhill. The path through the forest is flat. Have we gone off course? Or maybe the path isn't wide enough for skimobiles so we're taking a different route. I can't see where we are, thanks to a combination of the weather and the fact Rick's sitting right in front of me, his broad shoulders and tall frame, even when seated, blocking any view I might otherwise have.

I'm glad when we arrive at our destination, Schloss Schatten, and Rick helps me off the skimobile and removes my helmet and goggles.

Except it isn't Schloss Schatten I can see through the curtain of falling snow. It's Ritterherzburg.

I am so relieved I brought my camera.

'Surprise!' Rick says, smiling at me.

He takes my hand and quickly leads me out of the semi-blizzard, towards the castle. I look round at Marielle and the others and not one of them seems at all surprised. They must've all been in on the secret after all, not just Otto. Or perhaps they just knew the celebration was being held here.

Now I'm more convinced that the secret winter wedding is taking place tonight. You wouldn't hold a celebration here one night and then return the following day for a wedding ceremony, would you?

Or would you? I have no idea what the rich and famous might do.

We enter via the same door that my previous guided tour had taken, turn to the left and walk along a stone corridor that leads into a room similar to the armoury I'd visited. This room currently houses a row of modern coat rails with four attendants standing by, one of whom steps forward to take our coats and belongings. Rick helps me remove my coat before removing his own and I watch carefully to see exactly where the attendant puts my overnight bag. My camera is in there and I'll be needing that later.

'You look lovely,' Rick says.

'Thanks. So do you.'

He really does. Like Otto and Gunter, Rick is in full cowboy mode. He's wearing all black, including his studded cowboy boots and belt and he's just added a black, studded Stetson that our attendant handed him.

'What size are you?' Rick asks, glancing down at my fur-lined boots.

'Size 5. UK sizing. Why?'

He grins and points to a couple of rows of cowboy boots, all shapes, colours, and sizes, lined up on racks just a few feet from the coat rails. Just past those is a long, wide table on which sits a selection of cowboy hats from white to beige, to brown and black, made from a variety of materials from straw to felt to leather.

'Take your pick,' Rick says.

I choose a pair of white boots with glittering studs and he picks a matching hat and positions it perfectly on my head, teasing my hair into place beneath it, with his fingers. Then he points to a seat and, once I'm sitting, removes my own boots and slips on the white cowboy boots.

'They fit,' I say, laughing. 'I shall go to the ball.'

He winks at me. 'Yes ma'am. And you look mighty fine, Princess.'

His American accent is far better than mine, but his would be better, wouldn't it? He is an American, after all.

He takes my hand in his and leads me into a massive room I recognise from my guided tour. This is The Knight's Hall with its original heavy oak beamed ceiling, heraldic frieze, tiled floor, magnificent suits of armour, rows of leaded light windows, some containing stained glass, beneath which are stone window seats dotted with embroidered cushions, and the huge open fireplace at one end of the room, where there's now a roaring, log fire.

It seems Rick and Cody have friends who are country singing stars, and either they, or maybe Lucinda or her record label, have got a backing group, because at the other end of this long room is a stage on which the group is playing in support of a singer whose voice I definitely recognise. Behind them is a huge banner announcing who will be performing this evening, and it's a list of 'Country Greats'.

So much for a 'little celebration'. If this is their idea of little, I dread to think what one of their 'big' celebrations looks like.

But so far, we're the only guests here, other than Celestine and a few other people, none of whom I've seen before.

Celestine smiles and waves at us. She looks beautiful in a tan-coloured, fringed mini skirt and matching sleeveless fringed jacket. Her turquoise blouse, turquoise cowboy boots and matching hat are all dotted with rhinestones that glisten and gleam as she saunters towards us. I glance at Otto and I smile as his mouth drops open. He quickly closes it and pretends he's not interested but his gaze keeps drifting back in her direction.

'Hi y'all,' she says, with a wide grin.

It seems we're all attempting American accents tonight. This could get old, fast.

We exchange greetings as a waiter appears carrying a tray filled with glasses of champagne. Rick hands me a glass and I've never been so grateful for alcohol as I am right now. I've just spotted two people positioning what looks like a wedding cake as its three tiers, albeit three pink tiers, on a table near the middle of one of the side walls.

This is what I came here for. This is my big chance. This is the secret winter wedding. Lucinda and Cody are getting married tonight and not only will I get an inside scoop, I'm actually here by invitation! If you'd told me on Christmas Eve that things would turn out like this, I would've said you were insane. Miracles really do happen. And this miracle is happening to me. Right now. Right here.

I'm excited and nervous, guilty and terrified, thrilled and anxious, all at once, so much so that I've gulped my drink before Rick has said, 'Cheers'. He gives me an odd look and hands me another. Good thing the waiter is hovering right beside us. He must sense I'll be needing every glass he's got on that tray – and then some.

'What's going on, Rick?' I manage to ask. After all, I'm not supposed to know about this secret wedding so I need to behave as if I don't. 'I thought you said this was a little celebration. It looks like a special celebration to me. Is this an early New Year, thing? Or someone's birthday? Or what?'

He smiles. 'Can you keep a secret?'

I choke on my drink and it takes me a moment to pull myself together. Oh, if he only knew. But then again, it's a good thing he doesn't. I'd be out on my ear if he did.

'Are you all right?' he asks, clearly concerned.

I nod maniacally. 'Uh-huh.'

I gulp down the remainder of my champagne and he looks as if he's not sure what to do as I grab yet another glass from the waiter's tray.

'Are you sure?'

'Yep. Just ... nervous.'

He smiles reassuringly. 'Oh, sweetheart, there's no need to be.'

Now he looks as shocked as me. He obviously hadn't meant to call me 'sweetheart'. He reaches out for his second glass as I drink my third.

Marielle and the others are chatting just a foot or two away from us but it's as if they're not there and it's just Rick and me, who can't think of what to say or do next.

The expressionless and superbly professional waiter inches closer as though he knows we'll be needing more alcohol. Rick takes his third glass, hands me my fourth, taking the empty glass from me, and then clears his throat.

'Erm ... as I was saying, there's no need to be nervous. You're among friends.'

'Thanks. So ... what's this secret, then?'

The smile returns, and it's devastatingly gorgeous.

'Lucinda and Cody are engaged and this is their engagement party.'

He's sublimely happy. Me? Not so much.

'Engaged? That's it? Just engaged?'

Damn it. I shouldn't have said that. His smile is fading fast and doubt and questions are creeping into his eyes.

I hastily add, 'I mean ... *Just*, engaged? As in they've only *just* got engaged *today*? Oh my goodness! That's fantastic. I'm so happy for them.'

The doubt lingers for a second and then it's gone and he's smiling again.

'Yes. Officially. Although, between you and me, they've been engaged for a couple of months.'

'When's the wedding? I mean, they have set a date, right? If they've been engaged for a couple of months, I assume they have.'

'They have.' His eyes search my face.

'Don't tell me.' I smile at him. 'It's a secret, isn't it?'

'It is.'

'They like their secrets, don't they?'

He gives me an odd look. 'Don't you know who Lucinda is?' he asks. 'I thought you did and you were being considerate and treating her like a normal human being instead of the famous person she is.'

'Lucinda? Erm. To be honest, I did think she looks a lot like the pop star, Lucinda Revere, but I thought there was no way *that* Lucinda would be inviting me to dinner with her and her friends. I thought it must be a coincidence or something, and that she just looked a lot like her and had the same first name.'

I'm waffling and I'm not sure it's very convincing.

'No. She's *that* Lucinda. The famous one.'

'Oh. My. God! No way! You mean, I've had dinner with a Mega Star.' Now I've gone too far over the top. I need to get control. 'Wow. But then she's just a human being, like you and me, isn't she? So yeah. Even if I had known, once I'd got over the initial surprise, I would've treated her exactly the same as I treat everyone else.'

'I'm glad. We all hate all this celebrity nonsense. Especially Lucinda. She was so pleased when you didn't go crazy and fawn all over her. She really likes you, and the way you behaved that night made her feel you could be friends. You have no idea how happy that made me. Made all of us.'

'I'm glad too. Where are they then? Are they going to be making a Grand entrance?' I peer round him towards the door as more people arrive.

He laughs. 'Not a Grand entrance. But they will be waiting until a few more of their guests are here. And speaking of guests, there're a couple of people I should be saying hello to. Would you like to come with me, or would you rather not have to make small talk with people you don't know?'

'Would you mind if I stayed and chatted to Marielle?'

'No. I won't leave you for long, I promise. But I do have to perform some duties, as Cody's best ... friend.'

I smile. 'I completely understand.'

He almost said best man. So there *is* going to be a wedding. Yay! Thank God for that.

I wait until a few more people filter in and then I slowly wander across the room. The waiter moves away and serves other people with champagne.

I've got my phone in my handbag and I want to get a photo of the cake. If I position myself behind one of the suits of armour, I should be able to get a good shot of it. I would prefer to have my camera, but I can't hide that, so my phone will have to do. It's a decent camera on my phone, so it should still be okay.

No one seems to notice; they're all too busy chatting. I pretend to be looking at the armour and I slowly walk around it. I pull out my phone, take a few quick shots, and shove it back in my handbag, before strolling back to the front of the armour and then walking towards the stage. I'll get a few photos of that, and the banners showing who's performing here tonight. I'll take shots of the group and the singer on stage now, and then I'll take some photos of the room and the guests here so far. This is like a walk in the park. I had no idea it would be this easy.

I'm about to head back to Marielle and I'm still chatting to her when Rick comes to find me.

He slips his arm around me and smiles. 'I think it's time we had a dance, don't you?'

The music has changed slightly. It's still country, but it's jollier somehow and then I realise why.

'Can't I watch for a while first?' I plead, as he leads me by the hand to the middle of the room where a line of people has formed.

'Nope.'

He beams at me as Otto and Celestine join us, together with Marielle and a man I've seen somewhere before. I almost stumble as I realise where. It's from the photos on Tori's phone that she showed me on Christmas Eve. This man is Tori's boss!

The line starts moving and I lose count of the number of times I turn to my left instead of my right, or my right instead of my left, and bump into Rick or Otto.

I stomp on Rick's right foot at least three times by side-stepping in the wrong direction; by the fourth time, he is prepared for it and deftly moves out of my way.

When Rick takes my hand, holds our arms in the air, and spins me around, I almost fall over. And when I raise my leg, bend it at the knee and slap my ankle, I graze Rick's groin with my heel.

But that isn't the worst bit. Stupidly, I lean down as if to rub it better.

Fortunately, I stop myself before I touch him, and pull my hand away, but the look in Rick's eyes is a blend of shock, disappointment and amusement.

The line parts and people shift around and I find myself beside a total stranger who smiles at me forgivingly as I step on his toes.

'Sorry! It's my first time.'

'Don't you worry, little lady. We all had a first time once, and these here toes are made of steel. At least my boot tips are.' He's got a jolly laugh and a warm and friendly smile. 'Now you need to put your hand in mine and I'll dance you round the room a bit. Just follow my lead, and you'll do fine.'

'Thank you for being so understanding.'

I place my hand in his and try to keep pace as I scan the room for Rick who smiles and nods as we twirl past one another with our partners. He's with Marielle now, and I'm being twirled in every direction.

'I don't suppose these folks have had line dancing in this here castle before tonight,' the man says, with a look of pride.

'Perhaps not to this music.' For some reason I need to set the record straight. 'But the dances held in the 17th and 18th centuries weren't that dissimilar. Although not with the thigh slapping and the yee-haws. And the clothing was definitely different.' I smile as he spins me again.

'You don't say? Well blow me down, little lady.' His laughter is as jolly as he is.

It's not long before my new dance partner spins me back into Rick's arms and tips his hat with one hand before taking Marielle in his arms, and then they're gone, twirling and spinning, except Marielle keeps perfect time with him, and I step on Rick's toes yet again.

I'm just starting to get the hang on it when the song ends and everyone stops to clap and cheer and shout for more.

'I need some water,' I say. 'Line-dancing is almost as energetic as your muscle building workouts.'

Rick's eyes light up. 'Wanna sneak off and find somewhere private?' he asks with his American accent in full flow.

I raise my brows in mock horror. 'And end up in the prisoner's tower, for trespass? Or worse still, the torture chamber. I've been on the guided tour here. They've got both.'

'Then come out into the corridor with me for a second.'

I laugh. 'I'm not having sex with you in a corridor, no matter how tempted I may be.'

'Not sex. Just a kiss or two. I desperately need to kiss you right now.'

'Well, when you put it like that, how can I say no?'

He takes my hand and leads me out into the temporary, coat room and from there, towards the corridor where we entered. More people are coming in and several say hello to Rick. He smiles and says he'll see them later but there's something that requires his urgent attention, and we quickly pass through the crowds. Finally, we find a quiet place and he leans in to kiss me, pressing me against the wall which is cold against my back. I flinch.

'What's wrong?' There's concern in his eyes.

'It's cold.'

He grins, spins me around so that his back is against the wall and then he pulls me into his arms.

'Better?'

'Much better.'

He's just about to kiss me when heavy footsteps thump towards us around the corner. The next second, Cody appears. He's running so fast he nearly crashes into us. He's on his own, and for a newly engaged man, he looks miserable. Worse than that. He looks completely crushed.

Twenty-four

Rick darts a quick look at me and eases me away as Cody rushes towards us. Rick steps forward and Cody literally collapses against Rick's chest. All I hear Cody say is that something terrible has happened.

'What's happened?' Rick asks, grabbing Cody by both arms and holding him a little away so that he can see Cody's face. 'Has something happened to Lucinda? Where is she Cody?'

'It's lies,' Cody groans. 'All lies. But she's hurt and upset and ... and she says she needs time to think. I don't know what to do. I don't know what's happening.'

Rick glances at me again. 'You mean Lucinda's hurt? Physically hurt? Where is she?'

Cody shakes his head wildly. 'Not physically, no. Heartbroken. And it's my fault. But it's not. I didn't do it. I didn't. Why doesn't she believe me?'

'I don't understand. Are you saying Lucinda believes you've done something bad and she's told you she needs time to think? Are you saying she's not here?'

'Yes. She's here. But she's in the gate house. She won't come in. She told me to get Celestine. Celestine's not answering the phone. We've tried to call. I don't know what to do, Rick. I need your help.'

'I'll get Celestine,' I say. 'You stay with Cody.'

Rick nods. 'Thanks. We'll be outside. I think he needs some air to clear his head and I need to talk to Lucinda.'

I can see how worried Rick is but he's trying to remain calm. I dash back to The Knight's Hall, find Celestine and ask her to come with me. We hurry back to Rick and Cody as I tell her all I know, which isn't much.

'I think Lucinda may suspect Cody of cheating,' I say.

'What? Are you mad? Why would she do that?'

'I'll explain later. Rick said they'll be outside. Lucinda's in the gate house, I think.'

'Outside? Then we'll need our coats.'

I should've thought of that.

'I'll go back and get them and meet you outside.'

When I go back and ask for our coats, the coat attendant hands me my bag as I put my coat on. I start to say I don't need that right now but then I take it, just in case and strap it over my shoulder. If things go badly, we might end up going back to Schloss Schatten. I've got Rick's coat and Celestine's over my arm as I hurry towards the corridor.

When I get outside, I see Rick standing with Cody so I take Rick his coat first.

'Where's Celestine?'

'Thanks,' Rick says, taking his coat from me as he nods towards the gate house. 'She's in there with Lucinda. Let me know what's going on. Cody's still not making much sense. I think he's in shock or something.'

'It is a shock,' says Cody, as Rick puts his own coat on. 'I didn't do it. I'm sure I didn't. I love Lucinda. But if I did then … then I can't remember it and that's bad too.'

'I'll see what I can find out,' I say, and head towards the gate house.

I think I've got a good idea of what's going on but even I can't quite believe it. I think it has something to do with those messy girls and that photo of Cody I saw on that laptop. Somehow, Lucinda has either seen it, or been told about it, and she's having second thoughts about marrying a man she's just discovered is a cheat and a liar.

It doesn't take long for me to be proved right. But it's not quite what I thought.

Lucinda is slumped on a chair and Celestine is sitting beside her on another chair, with her arms wrapped around Lucinda's shoulders.

'You're saying someone handed you this envelope just now, right outside the castle gates and told you to look at it before you went inside?'

Celestine is clearly repeating what Lucinda has just told her, and Lucinda is crying.

'Y-yes,' Lucinda says.

'In front of Cody?'

Lucinda nods.

'And you're saying he said he is as astonished as you about what was inside it?'

Again, Lucinda nods but this time it's accompanied with a heart-rending sob.

Celestine looks up at me as I pass her coat to her and she retains eye contact for a few seconds before looking at Lucinda.

'Show Meg the photo,' Celestine says.

'I-I can't. It's too awful.'

'Was it a photo of Cody lying in bed with a woman and he's got his bandaged arm in the air as if he's trying to stop the photo being taken, but he's smiling?'

As I speak Celestine stares at me in disbelief and even Lucinda stops sobbing and looks me in the eyes.

'How do you know that?' Celestine asks, with an unpleasant edge to her voice.

'You-you've seen it?' Lucinda is horrified. 'When? How? You knew about this and you didn't tell me?'

'I only saw it by accident,' I say, trying to think of an explanation. 'And I wasn't sure what to do. I'd only met you the night before I saw it. And although I knew you were getting married, I don't know anything else about your relationship with Cody. Perhaps you've got an open relationship. Perhaps you knew he'd had sex with another woman.'

'So it's true? He did it? But you thought I knew? Do you really think I'd be marrying him if I … if I knew he'd cheated on me?'

'You might. People do.'

'Wait a moment,' Celestine says, now giving me a murderous look. 'How do you know they are getting married? Rick certainly hasn't told you. I know that for a fact. And Otto wouldn't. No one else knew about it other than me. And I haven't told a soul.'

'I … erm … does that matter now?'

'Yes. It does.' Celestine looks past me. 'Rick? Were you aware that Meg knew about the wedding? And what's more. She knew about this photo.' Celestine yanks the photo from Lucinda's hand and holds it in the air.

My heart sinks as I hear the sharp intake of breath right behind me and I slowly turn my head to see Rick standing there staring at me. So is Cody.

'You knew?' Rick looks as if I've stabbed him in the heart and twisted the knife for good measure. 'How?'

'No one knows except a few people we trust implicitly,' says Cody.

I let out a long sigh. I knew this moment would come. I just hadn't expected it to come so soon.

'I know I owe you all an explanation, but can we do this later? What's important right now is this photo. And whether it's true or not.'

'I think we need your explanation,' says Rick, taking the photo from Celestine and staring at it and then back at me.

'It's not true,' says Cody. 'I have never cheated on you, Lucinda. I love you.'

'What do you mean by "whether it's true or not", Meg?' Celestine demands.

There's a vacant chair and I flop onto it. I'm going to have to tell the truth and I won't be getting my inside scoop. But I do have a few photos and I will have this story. Plus, I've even got a photo on my phone, of the photo Rick is now holding, of Cody cheating, so I could use that. It's not as good as a wedding photo. But then again, there might not be a wedding.

'I haven't been entirely truthful about why I'm here,' I say. 'I haven't lied exactly, but I haven't told the truth. I know about the wedding because … because I work for a newspaper as a photojournalist and someone told me about it. So I came here hoping to get an inside scoop.'

'What!' Rick is furious. 'You did lie! And you used me! You used me to get to Lucinda and Cody!'

'I didn't! Not intentionally. It … it just seems that way now. But it wasn't like that. Honestly.'

'Stop!' Celestine shouts. 'This isn't about you two. This is about Lucinda and Cody and this photo.' She points to the photo Rick is holding and she grabs it back from him and thumps it in my lap. 'Explain.'

I drag my pleading look from Rick and glance at the photo.

'I can't explain the photo. Only how and when I saw it.'

'Do that now.' Celestine commands.

I tell them about that day and the messy girl's room, and every time I look at Rick, he looks away.

Cody looks bereft. 'I … I didn't cheat. I didn't. I don't know who the woman is. I've never seen her before, I don't think. And yet ... No. No it isn't. It can't be. I love you, Lucinda.'

We all look at him.

'You do know who it is, don't you?' I say.

He shakes his head and turns to Rick. 'No. Not unless. But that was years ago and there is no way I would've ever slept with her again. It can't be her, Rick, can it?'

'You do know her!' Lucinda screams.

'I ... I might.' Cody looks bewildered.

'Let me see the photo,' Rick says. Avoiding my eyes as I hand it back to him.

He studies it for what feels like ages but isn't really that long. A matter of a few seconds, perhaps, and then he slowly turns to look at Cody and even more slowly, he nods.

Twenty-five

'This is unbelievable,' Celestine says.

We have just established that the woman in the photo, in bed with Cody, is a girl Cody dated years ago when he and Rick first started competitive skiing. She lives in Aspen, or she did at the time, and they dated for about six months. Cody ended it when she started getting too intense and as his career was just taking off, he wanted to go on the ski circuit whereas she wanted him to settle down and get married.

'I was only nineteen,' Cody says. 'And we'd only been together for six months. She kept calling me or turning up at my folks' place, so I told her it was over and I left. A few years later, I saw her at one of the events I was competing in and we ... we hooked up again. Just for the night. I left the next day. After that, she kept turning up at events and kept saying it was a coincidence. We slept together a few more times but then it became obvious that it wasn't a coincidence. She was following me and my career. Going to where she knew I would be. And then, one night I was with someone else and she went crazy. I mean batshit crazy. She broke into my hotel room and completely destroyed it. I couldn't prove it was her but I knew it was. The next time I saw her I told her I'd get a restraining order against her if she didn't leave me alone. And in the end, that's what I had to do. I ... I haven't seen her since. But you can see why she would be the last person I would go to bed with. You have to believe me, Lucinda.'

'How do I know you're telling me the truth?' Lucinda says, but it's clear she wants to believe him.

'I can confirm it's all true,' Rick says. 'The woman was definitely crazy.'

'You would say that, wouldn't you?' says Celestine. 'You're his best friend so you'd lie for him if he wanted you to. You might've just made this all up while we were in here and you were out there talking. And the problem is, this is a recent photo. You're not nineteen in this photo. And you're wearing the bandage you wore after the accident in November. So this was taken in November. This November. Explain that.'

'She's right,' Lucinda starts crying again.

Rick and Cody look at one another and it's obvious they're trying to work out how this could be true.

'Hold on,' I say, getting to my feet and reaching out my hand. 'Give me the photo, please.'

Rick glares at me but gives me the photo.

'And tell me, Rick. Have you taken any photos of Cody since he had his accident?'

'Of course I have. Loads. What's that got to do with anything?'

'I mean, photos like this one.' I turn it around to show him. 'Photos of Cody in bed.'

Rick furrows his brows. 'No. Why would I do that? Especially if he's in bed with another woman. Not that I believe this happened. He wouldn't cheat on Lucinda. I know he wouldn't. We can't all lie as easily as you can.'

'I haven't ... Oh forget it. Just think. Are you absolutely sure? Not when you've been joking around? Saying you'll post it on social media, or something?'

'No. No way. As if I would do that when he loves Lucinda. What sort of man do you think I am?'

'You're not listening to me!' I say. 'Forget Lucinda. Forget the other woman. Look at the photo and imagine it's just Cody in that bed. Did you take a recent photo of Cody in bed? Alone.'

He looks at me for several seconds, as do the others.

'No. Not that I recall.'

I show the photo around. 'Did any of you take a recent photo of Cody in bed, on his own. Just Cody, remember. No one else. Celestine? Did you?'

'Me! Why would I be taking photos of Cody in bed, naked?'

'As a joke. To say you'll send it to Lucinda to show her he's lazy or something. I don't know. But I really think one of you did. And I think it might be you, Celestine. I think you might've had a few drinks and taken a photo, or something, and you don't remember. Just think. Better yet. Look at the photos on your phone. Because your phone went missing and was handed back and I think the person who took your phone is the person in this photo.'

Rick looks at me. 'Are you saying what I think you're saying?' He actually smiles at me, very briefly.

'I'm saying that this photo in my hand has been altered using photo editing software. And I'll explain why I think that, later, but please, Celestine, just look at your photos.'

'Are you saying Cody didn't cheat on me?' Lucinda looks hopeful. 'Because I can't believe you did, Cody, but ... but the photo ... it looks so real.'

'I didn't cheat on you, my darling. I never would. I just wish you would believe me.'

'Do it, Celestine,' Rick says. 'Because I think Meg might be right.'

Twenty-six

The music is still playing and the singer is in full voice; people are still dancing and drinking and chatting. Everything is the same as it was when Rick and I left to kiss and cuddle in the corridor, less than forty minutes earlier.

But everything has changed between me and Rick.

Apart from that brief smile in the gate house, he hasn't smiled at me since. He won't even look at me. And when I try to talk to him all he will say now is that there is nothing else to say.

But what he did say, before we came back in here was: 'We had fun. The sex was great. We both enjoyed it. But it was never going anywhere and it would've ended when you left in a few days, anyway. Of course, I'd have preferred it if you hadn't lied. If you hadn't used me to get to Lucinda and Cody. If you hadn't pretended to like me. If you hadn't made me feel that ... that you were a lovely person when in fact what you are is just someone who thinks it's okay to use people to get a leg up the career ladder. Just another journalist who wants to make a quick buck. Who doesn't give a shit about other people's feelings. We're done. I think you should tell Maria, Gunter, Marielle and Otto the truth, and if you don't I will – because I know they wouldn't have let you stay if they had any idea what you were up to – and then you should leave. And I mean leave GaPa. Today. Tonight. I'll even pay for your flight home to make sure you do.'

'Rick! Please! Let me explain.'

'What? So that you can lie to me again? No thanks. You made me think you cared about me when all you wanted was to get close to me so that you could get the inside scoop on Cody and Lucinda's wedding. You used me.'

'No! Well, okay. Maybe in the beginning. No. Not even then. I do care for you, Rick. I liked you the moment we met at Heathrow airport. It's been tearing me apart to keep this from you. But this is my career we're talking about. My future. This is what I do. This is what I love.'

'Hmm. I thought you loved photography. I thought you wanted to spend your life taking photos, not digging around to find dirt on people just to sell papers.'

'I want to work for magazines. Doing photoshoots or something. I want to travel the world.'

'And you're prepared to do anything to achieve that goal. Including sleeping with me.'

'No! I slept with you because I wanted to. I did that for me, not for my career. And what about you? Why did you sleep with me? To add another notch to your bed post? You don't have girlfriends. We didn't have a future, as you've just said. You were using me too. For a few days of fun. Nothing more. Nothing real. So don't you dare have a go at me. We are who we are.'

'I'm not sure I like who you've turned out to be. But good for you. You've got a story even though it's not the one you came for. I hope it brings you happiness.'

Then he turned and walked away.

So now I'm the one with the broken heart.

We proved that the photo was a fake. That it was edited. There was a photo of Cody on Celestine's phone. She still can't remember taking it, or why she did so, and Cody can't remember it being taken, but the photo on her phone shows the date it was taken and under the details section, it shows the time.

She took it at 1 a.m. in the morning, on Sunday December 4th, the day after they arrived at Schloss Schatten, not long after Cody's accident at Lake Louise, in Canada. Lucinda wasn't feeling well and so she and Cody had slept in separate rooms that Saturday night, so he wouldn't disturb her with his restless sleep.

The messy girls must have known Celestine would have photos of Cody on her phone as Celestine and Cody had been friends for six years, but the messy girls got lucky with that photo.

It was probably a spur of the moment thing. The girls discovered Celestine and Cody were friends; easy to do. You only have to look on the internet to see photos of them. Many of those photos were taken by Rick.

The messy girls used the editing software to paste one of them in, and they then printed out a photo of that and got someone to hand it to Lucinda as she arrived at the castle. Cody had said that the woman was effectively stalking him before. What he hadn't known was that she clearly hadn't stopped, despite the restraining order.

Lucinda and Cody are currently in another room of the castle, talking and making up, I suppose, and they'll soon be back on track, I'm sure.

Celestine thanked me for 'solving the crime' as she called it, but other than that, she too is ignoring me. It's as if I've got some deadly disease and need to be avoided at all costs.

I didn't tell any of them how I knew about the secret winter wedding – and I don't intend to, so Tori's job will be safe.

But I've had to tell Maria and Gunter and Marielle and Otto what I was really doing here, and that was very hard, because I genuinely feel as if I've betrayed their trust. They took it far better than I could've possibly hoped and they even hugged me.

'Perhaps, one day, you will come back and see us,' Maria said and Gunter seconded that offer.

'Or if you would ever like a job as a seasonaire,' said Marielle, 'you will be welcome to come and work with us.'

'No real harm has been done,' said Otto. 'And as you were the person who proved the photograph was fake, you should not feel too badly. When you return one day, I will teach you to ski.'

It made me rather tearful and I had to stop myself from blubbing. I told them Greta and Hugh knew nothing of my plan, because that's true, they didn't.

I hope Hugh and Greta aren't too cross with my brother when they find out. I can always say he didn't know either. In fact, I'm going to do that. I don't want anyone else's lives affected by my desire to get this story.

I just tried to talk to Rick again and to tell him how I truly feel but he walked away, and when I followed he turned and glowered and me.

'Do I need to get a restraining order on you? You're no longer here as my guest, and you're certainly not here as a friend of Lucinda's or Cody's so please leave.'

I hadn't realised he would be so cruel but I can see I have genuinely hurt him. Deeply hurt him. He may not do relationships, but friendships mean a lot to him and I've completely destroyed our friendship due to what he sees as my lies.

I take one look at The Knight's Hall before I leave. I even take one last photo on my phone. Rick sees me, and for a moment I think he's going to come over and take my phone from me, but instead, he turns his back.

And that's the last I'll ever see of Rick Price.

Do people die of a broken heart?

Because I think it's very possible I might.

Twenty-seven

I'm walking along the corridor on my way out when Lucinda and Cody appear in front of me. They are hand in hand but they look surprised to see me.

'You're leaving?' Lucinda asks.

I've got my coat on and my bag is on my shoulder and I've changed back into my fur lined boots so it's fairly apparent that I am.

'Rick has made it clear in no uncertain terms that I'm not welcome here. And I don't blame him. I'm truly sorry for deceiving you both. For deceiving all of you. I wish you both the happiness you deserve and I truly mean that. Goodbye.'

They step aside to let me pass and I'm fighting back the tears now.

'Wait, Meg.' Lucinda says, and when I stop she turns to Cody. 'Give us a minute, will you, Cody?'

He seems unsure but smiles at her. 'Anything for you, my darling.'

When he's gone she throws me a small smile.

'Thank you for helping us just now. If it hadn't been for you, I'm not sure what we would've done. I couldn't believe he would've cheated, and yet ... do we ever really know anyone? We have to trust our hearts. I nearly didn't. Rick is Cody's best friend, so I can't say you can stay. But I do hope that one day, we'll meet again, because I like you. I know they say you lied but I think you were just doing what you needed to do. And, although I'd rather you didn't, I can understand if you want to publish or sell whatever story you do have. Just tell the truth, please. I get so tired of reading things that have been made up.'

'I promise I won't lie. And thank you. That means a lot. I like you too, but I don't think we'll meet again. Good luck with everything though. I'm sure it'll be a wonderful wedding. I hope you'll be very happy.'

'I never wanted fame and fortune,' she says. 'I'll admit the fortune part is rather nice – but the fame part.' She lets out a small sigh and stares at a portrait painting on the wall. 'People think they know you even when they've never met you, or spoken to you. They think they have a right to know where you are, who you're with and what you're doing. They comment on what you wear –

from your make up to your clothes and everything in between. They comment on your choices. Your likes and dislikes. Sometimes it feels as if they think I'm a doll they can play with.' She looks directly at me once again. 'You don't realise how lucky you are, Meg. If I could live in a little seaside town with Cody and just live my life without all of this madness that follows us everywhere, I would. We both would. I'm just a small-town girl and Cody's just a small-town boy, who both love what we do. But neither of us love being in the spotlight.'

I can't believe how open and honest she's being. I can use all of this in my story.

'I can imagine it's tough. I've seen just how crazy your lives are from the stuff I've watched on the internet, and from what has happened here, and I'm not sure I could cope with it. In fact, I know I couldn't. But that's the price you pay, isn't it? There's no way out, is there?'

She lowers her gaze and colour creeps over her porcelain cheeks. My gut tells me I've just hit on something. Some secret she is trying to keep. A secret other than this wedding.

'Or is there?' I add.

A wistful sigh escapes her and she holds my gaze and then lets out such a long sigh she can't have any breath left in her body.

'You want a scoop, Meg. And after what you did tonight, maybe you deserve it. I can't let you come to the wedding. Rick is Cody's best man, and as I said just now, his best friend, but this will all come out and so will everything else, eventually. I'll tell you something that absolutely no one else knows, other than me, Cody, and Rick.'

'You will?' I can't believe my luck. A million questions pop into my head but I wait for her to continue.

'This was going to be Cody's last World Cup season, but, of course, he had to pull out after his fall. He'll make the announcement on New Year's Day, once we're married, so if you're really quick, you can get the story in print just as he's announcing it. He won't care. He's retiring from competitive sport and pursuing his other big dream. To teach kids from impoverished backgrounds about the joys of skiing. He's opening an academy, right here in this town, and providing free tutoring. And ... at the same time, I'll be taking a break from my career to spend more time with him.'

She smiles as she looks at me and although this is fantastic, I know that's not the whole story. There's another secret she's not ready to break. The reason she's tired. The fact she drinks water, not wine.

'You're having a baby, aren't you?'

She gasps, and I know I'm right.
Now I really do have an inside scoop.
This story could make me a fortune.
And it'll definitely help my career.

Twenty-eight

Valentine's Day is not a good day for single people. Especially not for those of us who have fallen in love with someone we will never see again and who will never return our love.

I can't believe I'm back at my old job, giving advice to future brides, and it's been over a month since I last saw Rick Price. Yet still, I wake up every morning, hoping I'll bump into him again one day. And he'll forgive me.

Huh. I should be so lucky.

I didn't sell Lucinda's story. Or Cody's. I didn't sell any photos. I didn't even mention anything in my bridal advice column or anywhere else in the local paper.

What I did do was write a travel article about the delights of GaPa and how spectacular the scenery is. I wrote about Zugspitze, Partnach Gorge and did research of other local beauty spots via Google. I recommended Chalet Maria as the best place to stay, or Schloss Schatten if you can afford it. I wrote about Ritterherzburg and why you might want to have your wedding there. And I said that one day, I hoped I would return because I had left my heart in Bavaria and I didn't think I'd ever get it back.

I toss the last pink balloon I've been inflating, onto the pile of other pink balloons waiting to be fixed together to form a heart-shaped arch. It'll be placed just inside the door of the Holy Trinity church hall for the Valentine's Day dance that is taking place here this evening.

Katie, Aaron, Tori, Emma and I foolishly offered to help decorate the hall, along with other people including Nan and Donald, and The Reverend Charles Chesterfield, and we've spent nearly all day doing just that. But right now I'm here alone because they've all gone off to do other things, like collect the food and drink, and one of us had to stay to blow up the balloons.

Aaron's taking Ember over to Mum and Dad's. They will be coming tonight but only for an hour or so as Ember won't mind being on his own for a short while.

Nan and Donald have gone home to change for this evening. It takes them longer to get ready than it does us youngsters, so Nan said.

The vicar's next door in Holy Trinity Church doing what vicars do at evening mass. It's been years since I've been to church, so I don't really have a clue, but every now and then the choir and the congregation burst into song. I try to sing along, except I don't remember the words to most of the hymns they're singing.

We're running out of time. It's already gone 6.30 and the dance begins at 8. p.m. so I hope the others get back soon. It'll take us a while to fix the arch. Fortunately, I took a break at 5 p.m. and was sensible enough to get changed then, so at least I don't need to dash home to get dressed. I'll just need to touch up my make-up and wash my hands. Not that I've got anyone to make myself look special for. Except myself.

I move over to the step ladder to hang a string of vivid pink, cardboard hearts that must've been forgotten. Aaron's fixed all the other strings of hearts in place. I could leave it until he returns, especially as I'm not a fan of step ladders, but this string doesn't need to be that high so I'm sure I can manage on my own.

Famous last words.

This step ladder is wobblier than I expected and I'm having second thoughts.

The front door of the church hall creaks open but I don't look round. I need to keep hold of this ladder or I might fall.

'Perfect timing,' I say to whoever it is. 'Come and hold this ladder will you, only I think it's come to life and is trying to shake me off.'

It must be Aaron because the hurried footsteps sound like a man's but when he speaks, it's not Aaron's voice.

'I think perhaps I should do that for you.'

I recognise the rich and sexy tone but I can't believe it's him. I spin round to look, completely forgetting I'm on a ladder. My feet get caught on one another and I sway for a second, arms flailing in the air, before I fall.

Rick catches me in his arms, and holds me there for a moment, before he eases my feet to the floor.

'What are you doing here?' I ask, without even saying thank you, but I am so astonished to see him and I'm wondering if I'm imagining the whole thing.

'Visiting someone,' he says, with an odd sort of smile, and a mixture of excitement and laughter dancing in his eyes.

'Visiting someone? Anyone I might know?' I brush my hands down my clothes, attempting to keep them busy so that I don't do something foolish, like throw my arms around him. I'm struggling to hide my emotions and I'm aware my voice is cracking as I speak. 'I wasn't aware you knew anyone in Norman Landing.'

'I know you.'

'Me? I suppose so. But you're not here to see me.' I look directly at him, a tiny beacon of hope flickering inside me. 'Are you?'

He beams at me. 'Aren't I?'

'Why?'

'I owe you an apology.'

I deflate like a balloon.

'An apology? You've come here to apologise?'

'Yes.'

'For what?'

'For being a jerk.'

I eye him curiously. There's something about his manner. His tone. The way he's standing. It's as if he's holding himself back and I'm not sure why.

'You could've done that by email. Or phone.'

'I couldn't.'

'Why not?'

'Because I wanted to see you.'

'To see me? Why?'

'I wanted to check if you're as beautiful as I remember. And you are. I knew you would be.'

'W-what?' Did I hear him correctly?

'And I wanted to ask if, perhaps, I could take you out to dinner?'

'To dinner? What for?'

'Well, for one, we both need to eat. For another, I want to spend some one-on-one time with you. But not just as a friend. And definitely *not* just as a hook up. I want to take you out. On a date. A real date. And to ask if you'll ever forgive me for the horrible things I said.'

'A ... a real date? Like, on a boyfriend, girlfriend kind of date?'

'Exactly like that. Yes.'

My entire body tingles and I almost squeal out loud with delight. Thankfully I don't. But I'm squealing inside and my heart is doing cartwheels.

'But ... but I thought you said you don't date. Ever. No exceptions.'

'I said a lot of things. Most of which I regret. And I did a lot of things I regret. The main one being, letting you leave the way I did. Telling you to go. Treating you so appallingly. That's my biggest regret. That, and not telling you how I felt about you. Not being honest with you ... or with myself.'

'You ... are you saying you have feelings for me?'

He nods oh so slowly and the smile on his lips is as sexy as hell. I'm thinking things I shouldn't be thinking in a church hall.

'I'm saying I've been an idiot,' he continues. 'I'm saying I'm sorry for the things I said to you that day. I'm saying that, even though I tried hard not to, I seem to have fallen in love with you. And that's a problem. A huge problem. Because now I need to know if you feel the same way about me. And it also seems that I can't stop thinking about you. I can't stop wanting to be with you. So here I am. Asking if you'll give me another chance. Being footloose and fancy-free doesn't make me happy now. In fact, I'm miserable. I don't want to be free and single anymore. I want to be with you. Wherever that may be. Even Norman Landing. The thing is, Meg, I love you. Really love you. Deeply. Passionately. What I feel for you is the sort of love that lasts a lifetime. No. Longer than a lifetime. Eternity. I don't want to live the rest of my life without you by my side. If you say no, I'll have to, but I'll be miserable. And I'll spend my time trying to win you back. So I'm wondering if you have any plans for, say, the next fifty, or sixty, or seventy years, and if not, could we make some plans together? And if you have, is it possible for you to change those plans to include me?'

'When would you like to start?' I ask, not quite certain that this is actually happening.

He reaches out his hand and I slip mine in his. He pulls me into his arms and smiles down at me with that dynamite smile of his.

'Right now. I'd like to start this second. I've already wasted six weeks being a fool.'

His lips meet mine in a kiss that is far beyond anything we shared before. When we finally part a fraction, I'm not quite sure where I am. I'm giddy and light headed and my legs might give way at any second, but thankfully, he's still holding me tight in his arms.

'Can I take that as a yes?' he queries, his voice cracking with emotion.

'That's a yes. Absolutely. I love you too, Rick. As deeply and as passionately as you love me. But just one question. What took you so long?'

He laughs. 'What can I say?' He kisses the tip of my nose. 'Some of us are fools and we don't recognise a good thing until it's gone. But if we're smart, we make sure we do everything we can to get that good thing back. I kept telling myself that it was just me. That you didn't love me. I kept thinking I could get over you and get on with my life. But I finally realised, I don't want to get over you. I love you. I adore you. I want you by my side. And now I've got you in my arms once more, Meg, I'm never going to let you walk away from me again.'

'I like the sound of that. Oh! But I can't go out to dinner tonight. I've got to be at this dance. There's a Valentine's Dance in this hall this evening.'

'I know.'

'You know? How?'

'Your colleagues at the local paper told me. That's how I knew you were here.'

'Oh, I see.'

It hadn't occurred to me to ask how he had found me. I only cared that he had.

'You could ask me to the dance,' he says, his eyes full of love and his smile full of promise.

'Then I'd be the one asking you out on a date.'

'That's true. Is that a problem?'

'Nope. Not at all. Will you come to the dance with me tonight, Rick?'

'What took you so long to ask?' he says, laughing. 'I love you with all my heart, Meg, and from this moment on, we'll be dancing through life together.'

'That sounds perfect. But you'd better make sure it's not a line-dance. I tend to kick you in the groin doing that.'

'Duly noted. But I can teach you all the steps you need to know and you'll soon be as good at that as you are at everything else. Which reminds me. I read your article on GaPa. It was excellent. You should consider being a travel writer. We could travel the world together. You could write and take photos and I'd continue my winter sports photography. Because together, you and I are the perfect team. In life. In love. In every way. What do you think?'

'I think that sounds wonderful. And I also think it's time you kissed me again.'

He does, and I believe every word he's said.

Because when you share a love like ours, nothing in the world can stop you from finding your happy ever after.

Coming soon

Visit www.emilyharvale.com to see what's coming next.

Plus, sign up for Emily's newsletter, or join her Facebook group, for all the latest news about her books.

Stay in touch with

Emily Harvale

If you want to be the first to hear Emily's news, find out about book releases, see covers and help pick titles or names of characters, sign up to her newsletter.

visit: www.emilyharvale.com

Or join her Facebook group for all of the above and to chat with others about her books:

www.emilyharvale.com/FacebookGroup

Alternatively, just come and say 'Hello' on social media:

@EmilyHarvaleWriter

@EmilyHarvale

@EmilyHarvale

A Note from Emily

Thank you for reading this book. I really hope it brought a smile to your face. If so, I'd love it if you'd leave a short review on Amazon, or even just a rating.
And, maybe, tell your friends, or mention it on social media.

A little piece of my heart goes into all my books. I can't wait to bring you more stories that I hope will capture your heart, mind and imagination, allowing you to escape into a world of romance in some enticingly beautiful settings.

To see my books, or to sign up for my newsletter, please visit my website. The link is on the previous page.

I love chatting to readers, so pop over to Facebook or Instagram and say, 'Hello'. Or better yet, there's my lovely Facebook group for the latest book news, chats and general book-related fun. Again, you'll find details on the previous page.

Also by Emily Harvale

The Golf Widows' Club
Sailing Solo
Carole Singer's Christmas
Christmas Wishes
A Slippery Slope
The Perfect Christmas Plan
Be Mine
It Takes Two
Bells and Bows on Mistletoe Row

Lizzie Marshall series:
Highland Fling – book 1
Lizzie Marshall's Wedding – book 2

Goldebury Bay series:
Ninety Days of Summer – book 1
Ninety Steps to Summerhill – book 2
Ninety Days to Christmas – book 3

Hideaway Down series:
A Christmas Hideaway – book 1
Catch A Falling Star – book 2
Walking on Sunshine – book 3
Dancing in the Rain – book 4

Hall's Cross series
Deck the Halls – book 1
The Starlight Ball – book 2

Michaelmas Bay series
Christmas Secrets in Snowflake Cove – book 1
Blame it on the Moonlight – book 2

Lily Pond Lane series
The Cottage on Lily Pond Lane – four-part serial
Part One – New beginnings
Part Two – Summer secrets
Part Three – Autumn leaves
Part Four – Trick or treat
Christmas on Lily Pond Lane
Return to Lily Pond Lane
A Wedding on Lily Pond Lane
Secret Wishes and Summer Kisses on Lily Pond Lane

Wyntersleap series
Christmas at Wynter House – Book 1
New Beginnings at Wynter House – Book 2
A Wedding at Wynter House – Book 3
Love is in the Air – spin off

Merriment Bay series
Coming Home to Merriment Bay – Book 1
(four-part serial)
Part One – A Reunion
Part Two – Sparks Fly
Part Three – Christmas
Part Four – Starry Skies
Chasing Moonbeams in Merriment Bay – Book 2
Wedding Bells in Merriment Bay – Book 3

Seahorse Harbour series
Summer at my Sister's – book 1
Christmas at Aunt Elsie's – book 2
Just for Christmas – book 3
Tasty Treats at Seahorse Bites Café – book 4
Dreams and Schemes at The Seahorse Inn – book 5
Weddings and Reunions in Seahorse Harbour – book 6

Clementine Cove series
Christmas at Clementine Cove – book 1
Broken Hearts and Fresh Starts at Cove Café – book 2
Friendships Blossom in Clementine Cove – book 3

Norman Landing series

Saving Christmas – book 1

A not so secret Winter Wedding – book 2

To see a complete list of my books, or to sign up for my newsletter, go to www.emilyharvale.com/books

There's also an exclusive Facebook group for fans of my books.
www.emilyharvale.com/FacebookGroup

Or scan the QR code below to see all my books on Amazon.

Printed in Great Britain
by Amazon

52339213R00158